The WALLS CAME TUMBLING DOWN

A Mystery Novel by
JO EISINGER

WILDSIDE PRESS

Chapter One

ROFILES ... A WAY OF LIFE ... *He is the best-hated man east of the Stork Club. His acidulous manner of expression and thinly disguised contempt for those about whom he writes has made him feared and disliked and the most sought-after person between Fifth Avenue and River House.*

His position as the café-society Nostradamus is secure, and his daily column in the Morning Post, *signed simply "D'Arcy" (he has quite forgotten that he ever had another name), retails in biting style the latest erotic hodge-podges of that set ...*

It is no secret that D'Arcy looks upon his work merely as a not-too-unpleasant means to an end; it permits him to live his kind of life. He has a positive mania for looking after his own well-being; and at the slightest indication that some situation or person might disturb the even tenor of his existence, he flees like a stag from hounds ...

I raised my bulk from the couch in my private office at the *Morning Post* and threw the copy of *The Gothamite* which I had been reading clear across the room. I was in a pink fury.

Seething inwardly, I took up the telephone and started to dial the number of the magazine, but before a connection could be effected, I hesitated, slowly replaced the receiver on the prong, and sat for a long moment in thought.

No, it was not a particularly flattering portrait which *The Gothamite* had drawn of me. But how could I complain? Certainly it did square with the public conception of D'Arcy, and it was a conception, I had to admit, which I had deliberately nurtured through the years.

I lay back on the couch and started to dictate into the machine when the door to the anteroom opened and Susan looked in hesitantly.

Susan is my devoted secretary. Seeking a girl yet uncorrupted by years of rigid training and discipline in some business organization, I had plucked her bodily out of a school of stenography, intending to mold her to fit my scheme of things. But I soon learned that Susan had a mind like a steel trap. Apparently, it had been slammed shut in her tenderest infancy, and nothing on God's green earth would ever pry it open.

"Well, girl — what is it?" I asked testily.

Susan swallowed hard and ran her tongue quickly over her dental brace.

"There — there is someone outside to see you, sir," she said.

"Susan, my pet," I said patiently, "how often have I told you that I am not to be disturbed while I am working?"

"I told him you're very busy, Mr. D'Arcy, but he just won't go away."

"Oh, God!" I groaned. "If it's someone with a bit of malicious gossip, tell him to mail it to me. And for heaven's sake, Susan, please don't whine in that key!"

"I'm not whining, sir. And I don't think he has any malicious gossip. It's a priest."

I looked up at the girl in surprise.

"Did you say a priest, Susan?"

"Father Walsh. And he says it's very important and you *must* see him."

I thought for a moment and was quite certain I had never heard the name before. I spun my mind back quickly over my columns of recent date and was further certain that I had written nothing which might have offended the Church.

"Very well, Duchess. Ask Father Walsh in."

Susan smiled gratefully and went out. After a moment, the door opened slowly and Father Walsh peered into the room.

He was a small man with a great many years to his credit, and he wore his age with charming grace. The finely textured, almost transparent skin of his face and hands adhered lightly but firmly to his small, fragile bones, and his startlingly luxuriant silver hair gave him an air of great benignity.

I rose to greet him. "Please come in."

For another brief instant, he stood on the threshold and blinked at me uncertainly. Then he nodded his thanks, closed the door gently behind him, came into the room, and lowered himself carefully into the least comfortable chair in the office.

"You are Mr. D'Arcy?"

I said: "Yes. I am D'Arcy." And then, as he did not speak: "What can I do for you, Father?"

The aged priest settled back in his chair and smiled. I could feel a certain tension leave him as he gazed into my eyes, and he nodded his head slowly, as though really recognizing me for the first time.

"Yes, yes," he said softly. "My, you've changed. But of course . . . it's been so many years . . ."

The low, throaty whine of a river tug leading a blind steamer into the bay reached my ears faintly. It was that sound which released the flood of memories, and then I knew.

Father Walsh: the priest of the parish in which I had lived as a child!

I had not seen Father Walsh for more years than I liked to remember, and in the instant which followed recognition, a wave of long-buried memories washed over me:

It had been a rather mean section of the city, Father Walsh's old parish, on the westernmost fringes of Greenwich Village, and the foghorns of the river had been as much a part of my youth as the nightly thrashings at the hands of my beer-sodden father.

Sitting there in my office with Father Walsh before me, however, the not-so-tender days of my youth, and life with a family of six in a cold-water flat of four rooms, seemed to take on a roseate glow and a warmth which, of course, they never possessed.

I went to him at once and took his hand in mine.

"Oh, I'm so glad to see you!" I exclaimed inadequately, and I was struck by the note of sincerity in my voice. I had not heard that for a long, long time.

He said: "Thank you, D'Arcy. And I don't think I need tell you what great pleasure this gives me, too, It brings back so many memories . . . memories of . . ."

I ran my fingers lightly across that small scar over my left eyebrow, and Father Walsh's smile widened.

"It will always be with you — eh, D'Arcy?"

I smiled ruefully.

"Indeed it will, Father, and a good thing, too; a constant reminder that 'crime does not pay'; and," I added, "a constant reminder of your goodness."

Father Walsh waved a deprecating hand.

"I did nothing, D'Arcy. You just needed understanding and guidance when you became involved with those older boys and that trouble with the police. . . ."

"But if it hadn't been for you, Father, my life from then on might have been entirely different. My own father, you remember, was quite ineffectual. But if *you* hadn't spoken to the authorities, well . . . And I feel like an absolute dog for not having visited you all these years."

"Please don't berate yourself, my son. I know that we all have our lives to lead, and you've succeeded in making yours in a world which is — well, just a bit alien to me."

"I don't know," I said. "I sit here talking to you and I wonder if I really am a success. . . . But never mind. Tell me about yourself. Are you still in the same parish, the same church?"

"Yes," he sighed, "the same old neighborhood, the same old church — and I think I love it all now more than ever: the church, the people. But —"

He broke off abruptly. A cloud seemed to pass across his face. I could see that something weighed heavily on his mind.

"What is it, Father?"

"D'Arcy, I know that you are a very busy man —"

"Nonsense! I've always time for —"

"But I don't know where else to turn," he went on. "I — I've come to ask your help."

"But of course! You know I'd do anything to help you." And then, as he hesitated: "Are you having trouble?"

"It — well, it's a strange story, my son. And even now I'm not sure that — but you must believe that what I tell you is the truth."

"I've never known you to speak anything but truth, Father."

"But this —" He stared down at the carpet, clearly loath to continue. After a moment he looked up into my face slowly, and there was a new apprehension in his eyes. "It was three nights ago, late in the evening, when he first came."

"Who?"

"A man I'd never before seen nor heard of. My housekeeper was not at home, and I answered the door myself. I invited him into my study, and when I asked what I could do for him, he said that if I were really Father Walsh, his search was ended; he had been seeking me for a long, long time. . . ."

"Seeking you?"

"Those were his words. I asked him why he wanted me, and he said he had come for the Bibles."

"What Bibles?"

"I don't know. And when I asked, he smiled as though we were playing some sort of game and said: 'The Bibles marked *E. B.*'"

"*E.B.?*" Did that mean anything to you?"

"Nothing, D'Arcy. And when I told him so, his face grew — well, menacing is the only word, I suppose, as though his patience were at an end."

"Did he identify himself?"

"No."

"In no way at all?"

"Not a word. He asked me if I were dealing with anyone else for the Bibles. I again told him that I didn't know what he was talking about, and when I suggested that perhaps he'd better leave, he rose from his chair in anger, saying that I would help him find the . . . find the —"

The flow of words stopped abruptly.

"The Bibles?"

"No," whispered the priest. "No, not the Bibles . . .

That I would help him find the — Walls of Jericho, or else I would regret it!"

The aged priest was breathing heavily.

"Did you say the — Walls of Jericho?"

"Yes. And then he left as suddenly as he had come."

"Why, that's incredible! And have you seen him since?"

"Yes."

"He visited you again?"

"No. But for the past two nights he's been loitering outside the gates of the churchyard."

"Have you reported this to the police?"

"I can't go to the police, D'Arcy."

"You — I don't understand."

"I've been warned not to."

"By this man?"

"No. By my Bishop. I reported the incident to my Bishop after the first visit, but he refused to believe me. He accused me of — of growing senile . . . said it was all a figment of my imagination, warned me never to speak such nonsense again."

I regarded the priest narrowly.

"Yes . . . I see . . ."

"Well, I tried to put the entire thing from my mind, but since seeing him watching the house these past two nights, I decided to speak with you."

I tried to keep the growing awareness out of my eyes and the sadness from my voice.

"Yes, Father. I'm glad you did."

For a moment the priest looked at me anxiously, and there was a pleading in his eyes. It was not a pleasant thing to see him sitting before me with his mind, which I remembered had been always so sharp and alert, entering its senescence.

I hesitated before speaking. Then I said: "Father, before we do anything about this, you must promise one thing: you will not worry and you will not go to anyone else. You must leave it all to me. And I am sure you have nothing to fear."

"Oh, I see! You — you don't believe me either."

Father Walsh smiled wanly, a look of pain in his eyes.

I said quickly: "Father, I do believe you," but it

sounded horribly glib, and I hastily added: "Please let me visit you tonight. We'll talk more about it then. I want to sit and talk with you about — about many things . . . as we did years ago . . ."

Father Walsh sighed deeply as he rose from the chair. He smiled wearily and held forth his hand.

"Yes, D'Arcy. Years ago — I'll expect you. And — thank you."

I took his hand, and then he turned and left as quietly as he had come, closing the door softly behind him.

For a long time after the priest had gone, I sat perfectly still. Seeing Father Walsh at this time had disturbed me deeply. I now found myself looking forward with impatience to spending the evening with the aged priest. It was the only way in which I might, for a brief time at least, bathe in the warm waters of the past.

I sighed deeply as I took up the telephone and dialed a number. After a moment, a voice said hello and I said:

"René? D'Arcy. Sorry, but I can't possibly make the theater tonight."

The Count René de Brisseaux had always toyed with the small conceit that we were close friends.

René said: "Oh, but I say, D'Arcy! The Countess, you know, is depending upon you. This is the benefit for her organization fighting against tuberculosis!"

I said: "You may tell the Countess that I've decided to fight on the other side."

I put the telephone away and returned to my work.

THE CAB DREW AWAY and I stood for a moment on the curb. My eyes finally pierced the thick gloom surrounding St. Francis's. Faintly I could discern the outlines of the buildings on the other side of the high iron fence.

The iron-filigree gate of the church grounds fronting Grove Street stood ajar, and I slowly entered.

I lifted the ancient, heavy brass knocker of Father Walsh's residence and made my presence known. There was no response; I pushed the door open and entered the musty, dimly lighted hall.

I called out for Father Walsh, but there was no answer. I drifted into the study. Huddled there on a chair in a corner of the room, face white with shock and eyes filled with terror, was an aged woman.

A dark foreboding gripped me as I went to her side. "What happened?"

She did not speak, but pointed a shaking hand to a small room off the study. I strode quickly to the door, and then stopped abruptly. Suspended from a low beam in the ceiling, the cord of his robe knotted tightly about his neck, Father Walsh swayed gently to and fro. I could see at once that there was no urgent need to cut him down. Father Walsh was quite dead.

The sound of the front door being slammed shut startled me, and I turned to see three men enter the room. They were Captain of Detectives Fred Griffin and his two aides, Regan and Lucas.

Griffin, a spare, thin-lipped, taciturn man, halted abruptly when he saw me.

He said: "You're D'Arcy of the *Post*."

I was still deeply shaken, and in an effort to regain my composure, I lit a cigarette before answering.

I said: "The *Morning Post*. And you are Captain Frederick Griffin of Homicide."

Griffin asked: "What are you doing here?"

I said: "It certainly did not take you gentlemen very long to arrive. Do you have a divining rod for corpses at headquarters?"

"The housekeeper called and said that —" He broke off. "But where do you fit in?"

"I don't."

Griffin scowled and went into the small library and made a quick, superficial examination of the body. He looked about the room, noted the small footstool overturned near the priest's feet, and came back into the study and turned to the woman.

"You're the housekeeper?"

"Yis, yir honor."

"What's your name?"

"Brigid, yir honor. Brigid Corr."

"All right, Brigid. Tell me what happened."

"I — I don't know, yir honor. I came in here to give

the Father his warm milk. He was not in the room and I thought likely he must be poking about in the book room like he sometimes does — did. And so I went in to call him, yir honor, and thin I saw ... thin I saw ..."

The woman broke into sobs, rapidly making the sign of the cross again and again. Griffin was impatient.

"All right, Brigid. Then you called the police?"

"Yis, yir honor."

"And then what did you do?"

"I called his rivirince, the Bishop?"

"You called the Bishop?"

"Yis, yir honor. I called his rivirince and told him that Father Walsh, God rest him, was hanging from the ceiling. His rivirince said he'd be right over."

Griffin turned to me.

"All right, D'Arcy. Give."

"Very little I can tell you, Captain. I just happened to drop by for a chat, and I found this."

Griffin asked sarcastically: "And you're in the habit of dropping by for chats with priests?"

The knocker on the front door clanged loudly. Regan went quickly, and there was a brief silence until he returned with Bishop Roger Martin.

A tall and aloof individual, Bishop Martin fairly exuded authority, austerity, and dignity from every pore. His tones rolled forth as though he were in the pulpit. "You are the police, I take it."

Slightly disconcerted by the Bishop's authoritative manner, Griffin admitted that he was indeed the police.

"I am Captain Griffin of —"

"Yes. Quite," the Bishop interrupted, his eyes falling on the housekeeper. "Ah, if you are through questioning this woman for the moment, I'd like you to dismiss her. There is something I must tell you."

With ill-concealed reluctance, the housekeeper shuffled into the hall. Lucas closed the door behind her and then stood by silently, his hand on the knob.

"Now as to this — this unfortunate —" The Bishop gestured with an expressive hand. "I don't mind confessing that I am deeply shocked, of course; but I am afraid it has not come to me as any great surprise. I feared that something like this might very well happen. I am afraid that Father Walsh suffered a — a temporary — ah, dementia, and so took his life."

"And what makes you believe that?" Griffin asked.

Bishop Martin hesitated, then spoke slowly, as though carefully selecting his words.

"Frankly, I am most reluctant to speak of this, and purely out of consideration for, ah, for Father Walsh's memory, I would deem it a favor if little of what I say were to be included in your report. Of course, I fully realize that the death must, unfortunately, be set down as suicide. But could it not be said that it was suicide brought about by ill-health rather than —"

The Bishop left the implication hanging in midair.

Griffin looked down at the floor as he fingered his lower lip, but glanced obliquely at the Bishop through his left eye, the shrewd eye. Then: "You can count upon my co-operation to — well, to make things as easy as possible for all concerned."

"Thank you, Captain," said Bishop Martin.

Griffin grunted.

"*Ummm.* Yes. Well, now, what makes you think it was suicide?"

"The truth is, Captain, that a few days ago, Father Walsh came to me with a most fantastic tale: He insisted that he had been visited by some strange creature who demanded his help in finding the Walls of Jericho."

"I beg your pardon?"

"Exactly. The Walls of Jericho. He said that he had been threatened and seemed in great fear."

"One moment, sir. You mean, some man came to Father Walsh and asked him to help him find the Walls of Jericho — the biblical Walls of Jericho?"

"Precisely. He told me that at first this strange person had demanded the Bibles, but what Bibles he could not explain. Of course, I saw at once that he was suffering an aberration. He had always been a fervent student of the Bible and had always been deeply impressed by the story of Joshua. It was quite clear that it had temporarily affected his mind.

"I reprimanded him rather strongly," continued the Bishop, "thinking to shake this hallucination from his mind. I told him he must never again speak such non-

12

sense, and that if he persisted, I would be forced to suggest his retirement."

I said: "And that's what I thought when he visited me."

Griffin turned to me sharply.

"When who visited you?"

I told him of Father Walsh's sudden call.

"And that is why I am here," I went on. "I saw that his mind was a little rocky. I tried to humor him, promised I would visit him tonight — and here I am."

Griffin said: "Well, I guess that sews it up. Regan, take care of the report for the Med. . . . All right, D'Arcy, you can go now. But make sure you don't get into the habit of being found with stiffs. It's very unhealthy."

I started down the hall, glad to be on my way. I reached for the outer door, but before I could open it, the brass knocker again clanged its summons. I swung the door open and stood face to face with a woman.

She was young, somewhere in her earlier twenties, and even in the gloom it was evident that she was very beautiful.

"Yes?" I said.

"Father Walsh is expecting me," she said.

By now Griffin had come quickly down the hall, and before I could speak he elbowed me aside and confronted the girl. Behind him was Regan.

"Come inside, please," said Griffin.

The girl looked at the men with her large eyes, and it was then that I thought I detected a faint flicker of fear in them, but it was gone as quickly as it had come — if, indeed, it had been there at all.

Griffin flashed me a look which can only be described as baleful. "You'd better go now, D'Arcy."

I descended the dark steps slowly, walked through the silent church grounds, crossed the street, and took up my stand in a shadow-filled doorway.

I did not have very long to wait. The door to Father Walsh's residence opened, a thin shaft of light cut across the darkness and disappeared. The girl came down the stairs.

She left the church grounds and looked up and down the street for a taxi, then walked slowly to the corner. I followed on my side of the street, and when, in answer to her signal, a cruising cab drew up before her, I crossed quickly to her side. Before she could reach for the door, I swung it open and waited for her to enter.

I did not, of course, really expect her to do so, but I was mistaken. She looked up into my face for an instant, then a slow, charming smile crossed her lips and she moved into the taxi.

I followed her in, closed the door, gave the driver his instructions, and we sped off.

THE RIDE THROUGH the narrow, winding streets was brief, and a few minutes later our cab drew up before Bianca's Neapolitan Restaurant. Bianca's was one of the innumerable basement dining rooms which dot Greenwich Village. It had been there for many years, and was regarded as virtually an institution in that section of the city.

During the ride I had introduced myself to the girl, but she volunteered no information about herself, not even her name. She had been pleasant enough, but seemed content merely to sit back and listen to me talk.

"I'm afraid I've acted quite on impulse coming to your cab this way," I said. "I do hope you will forgive me."

I waited for her to speak, but she simply inclined her head slightly and smiled in answer.

During the remainder of the ride, I desisted from further talk, confident that a bottle or two from Bianca's wine-cellar would soon lubricate the mainsprings of her tongue.

When we entered the basement restaurant, Bianca came forward, upper part of his stocky torso bent back, both hands flung forward, and a broad, beautiful, radiant smile on his fleshy face.

"Meester D'Arcy!" he sang out happily. "Is so good to see you again, no?"

There was an infectious warmth and sincerity about Bianca, and I liked to flatter myself by thinking that he would have been just as pleased to see me even if I were not D'Arcy of the *Morning Post*.

14

"Well, you're looking happy and healthy, Bianca," I smiled.

Bianca led us to the rear of the restaurant.

"You stay 'way a longa time, no? Maybe you find other place for better *Lasagna*, yes?"

Bianca cocked his head to one side and waited for the routine compliment.

"When better *Lasagna* is made," I said pontifically, "I will eat it at Bianca's."

Without further ado, I told Bianca what we desired in the way of food and wine, and off he went into the kitchen to see that our dishes were properly prepared. I turned my attention to the girl.

"What is your name?" I asked abruptly.

"So you're *D'Arcy*," she said without answering my question.

"Right. And you are . . ." I was insistent.

"Rebecca. I despise it. But all my friends call me Rachel."

I took up the bottle of *Lagrima Christi* which Bianca had brought to the table and held it over her glass.

"Just to the top of the glass, please," she said.

I poured the wine carefully.

"And what is the rest of your name?" I asked.

"Fothersgill. Rebecca Fothersgill."

"Fothersgill," I murmured. "I once knew a Fothersgill."

Bianca's beaming face emerged through a cloud of steam and tempting odors as he brought our food to the table.

"*Lasagna a la Bianca!*" he sang out. "With for you, Meester D'Arcy, the special *mozzerella* cheese!"

While I enjoyed the excellent dish, "Rachel," barely touching hers, continued to drink nervously and almost at forced draught. I replenished the wine in her glass as rapidly as she drained it.

"Yes," I said, taking a fresh bottle from the bucket at my feet, "my Fothersgill was the manager of a bank. A long time ago. In Paris. . . . I suggest we drink this one to the memory of Father Walsh."

The girl hesitated with the glass to her lips, then slowly sipped the wine.

"Did you know him well?" I asked quietly.

15

The girl looked up sharply.

"Who?"

"Father Walsh."

For an instant she sat in silence, twirling the stem of her glass in her fingers. Then she asked cautiously:

"How well did you know him?"

"Slightly," I lied. "I was merely helping him to organize a charity affair."

"Yes," she said softly. "He was a very charitable man. I shall always remember him for that."

"Where did you meet him?"

"Oh, I met him," she said vaguely. "Yes, it was a long time ago. He was very kind to me."

Apparently she had decided upon her answer, and there was nothing for it but to play along.

"He was kind to everyone," I replied.

"Why, he was practically a second mother to me," she went on a bit more rapidly. "Yes, actually a second mother."

She was now being *tragique* in the grand manner (a tribute, indeed, to Bianca's wine) and sat for a moment in brooding silence. Then she rambled on between drinks, telling a completely mad story about her early life in China, and of how her mother had run off with a Chinese merchant and how her father followed them in a junk and killed them both, for which act of violence he was duly beheaded, and it was then that Father Walsh, who ran the Christian Mission in Peiping, took her to live in the mission.

"And now," she continued, "he too is dead. I traveled all this way to see my second mother once more, and now he's dead. Isn't it beastly?"

"So that's how you came to Father Walsh?"

"Yes."

A wandering artist came to the table with his sketch pad and asked if he might draw the girl's picture, and as he worked, she asked what he was doing and I told her that I should like a sketch of her as a memento of our first meeting. She said that that was a nice thought and that she was very flattered and in a few minutes the artist finished an excellent likeness and I gave him a bill and he went away. I asked "Rachel" to sign her name to it as a token and she said of course as she took my pencil and signed "Rosemary Fortescue." I thanked her solemnly and folded the sketch and put it in my pocket and she said she hoped it would give me some sort of consolation. I suggested that she might be able to find some consolation in the Bible and she looked up at me sharply and repeated the Bible? and the mist cleared from her eyes slowly like dew drying under a hot morning sun. They were suddenly sharp and alert as she rose to her feet and said that she had to go. I helped her on with her light coat and noted the label from the swank San Francisco shop and then I paid the bill and promised Bianca I would return soon.

We went out into the street where a cab was waiting but she would not let me take her home. Suddenly she put her arms about my neck and pressed her warm moist lips to mine. The bored cab driver opened the door for her and she got in and I took one of my cards from my case and put it into her hand and told her that she could come to see me at any time, at any time at all, and we would talk about Father Walsh and we would talk about the Bibles and that is when I saw her face go pale. Then her cab sped off and I stood for a moment watching it down the street and out of sight, still feeling her lips on mine. . . .

I went back into Bianca's and asked him for an envelope and across its face I wrote: Mr. John Barrett, San Francisco *Ledger*, San Francisco, California." Then I took the sketch of the girl from my pocket and placed it in the envelope and sealed it and put an airmail stamp on it which Bianca also gave me, and then went out into the street and dropped the envelope into a mailbox.

I returned to the restaurant, deposited a coin in the telephone on the wall, and dialed a number. After a moment, a voice on the other end said:

"Police Headquarters."

I said: "Captain Griffin, please."

I waited for the connection to be made, and then I heard Griffin's voice:

"Griffin speaking."

"This is D'Arcy, Captain Griffin."

"Oh."

"Captain, I must talk to you."

"What about?"

"Father Walsh. I've reason to believe he might have been telling the truth."

"About that visitor and the Walls of Jericho?"

"Yes. I've just been with that girl."

"What girl?"

"The one who called at the house when I was leaving. I don't know her name. She told me an obviously fantastic story about herself and Father Walsh, and when I mentioned Bibles, she seemed to react rather strongly."

"You think Father Walsh was murdered?"

"I'm beginning to believe that, yes."

"Now look here, my friend," said Griffin, "I kind of expected this call from you. I won't have this thing dirtied up! The poor old priest was soft upstairs — and as far as my office goes, the case is marked suicide and closed. I've talked to the press, and the boys are being decent about it. They're going to play it down out of respect for the priest's memory. I asked them to do that. But I'm not asking you. I'm *telling* you! Lay off it, D'Arcy."

Griffin severed the connection with a venom that crackled through the wires.

I deposited another coin and dialed the number of the *Morning Post,* and after a moment heard:

"City desk."

I said: "Nick? This is D'Arcy. You'll be getting a story about the suicide of a priest named Father Walsh. I want a favor on that, Nick."

Nick said: "Sure. What is it?"

I said: "I'd like the lead to read that I discovered the body and was on the scene when the police arrived."

Nick said: "Lot of people going to think it kind of screwy: D'Arcy having anything to do with priests — dead or alive."

I said: "That's exactly what I am counting on."

I hung up and headed for home.

Chapter Two

HE TELEPHONE by my bed rang. I thrust my hand out from beneath the warm sheets and groped for the phone.

"Hello!"

"This is the desk clerk, Mr. D'Arcy."

"At this hour? What time is it?"

"I'm terribly sorry, sir, but there is a gentleman here to see you."

"A gentleman?"

"He said you would be expecting him and he insisted I ring you. A Reverend Probiloff."

"Who?"

"Reverend Probiloff. Shall I send him up, sir?"

"I don't . . ." And then: "Yes. Five minutes."

I was slipping into my robe when the door-buzzer sounded.

"Come in."

The door opened, and the Reverend Probiloff made his entrance. He was very tall, very thin, very dour. He had the long, lean face and dark, sunken eyes of the ascetic or the fanatic. Under his arm was folded a fresh newspaper.

"You are Mr. D'Arcy?"

"Yes."

The Reverend Probiloff closed the door behind him and seated himself in the most comfortable chair he could find.

"I must ask you to forgive this early call," he said. "But it is most urgent that I speak with you as soon as possible."

My visitor smiled at me in what, I suppose, he considered an engaging manner.

"May I introduce myself? I am the Reverend Sergei Probiloff."

"Precisely what you told the desk clerk."

"Yes . . . I am a missionary."

"And have I been recommended as a prospect?"

The Reverend Sergei Probiloff laughed politely.

"Perhaps I should have said an ex-missionary. During most of my life I've served God all over the world. But because of my failing health, I was forced to retire — and most reluctantly — from this noble work. That was some years ago. Since man, however, cannot live by bread alone, I devoted myself fully to my hobby. I am an amateur bibliophile. I specialize in collecting rare Bibles."

The Reverend Sergei Probiloff broke off, reached into his waistcoat, and drew forth a silver cigarette case. "But to the problem at hand: There are two Bibles of a certain edition which I must have to complete the collection on which I am now working. They are quite old and, if my information is correct, the covers are stamped with the initials *E. B.* After an exhaustive search, I determined that these Bibles were in the possession of a priest named Father Walsh . . . Yes, a priest named Father Walsh . . . I am prepared to pay well for those books, Mr. D'Arcy."

The Reverend Sergei Probiloff's voice trailed off into complete silence.

I said: "Your unexpected visit has been delightful. Indeed, these few moments shall remain among my treasured memories. And now, my dear Reverend, permit me to wish you every success in your hunt for the Bibles."

I started for the door. His voice checked me.

"You are dismissing me?"

"In a word: Yes?"

"Does my story not hold interest for you?"

"Other than to indulge yourself in labored verbal gymnastics, you have said nothing and told me nothing."

"You are quite right, Mr. D'Arcy," Probiloff said, that small, snide smile playing quickly across his lips.

"As I think back, I see that I have really told you nothing. You have been very patient with me, and I am not ungrateful. In the future, I am sure, you will find that — "

"What do you want?" I interrupted curtly.

I had stepped close to him, and now stood directly before him, towering above his chair.

"I want those Bibles," he said quietly.

I settled back on my heels. Now it was out.

"Why come to me?"

Probiloff took the newspaper from under his arm and held it forth. It was a copy of the *Morning Post* and his finger rested on a story, set under a one column head, on the lower half of page one. Nick had done as I had asked:

PRIEST'S DEATH
DISCOVERED BY
SOCIETY WRITER

The body of Father James Walsh, priest of St. Francis' Church in lower Greenwich Village, was discovered hanging from a beam in his library late last night by D'Arcy, columnist for the *Morning Post*. . . .

"You see, Mr. D'Arcy," Probiloff's voice droned on as I read the news item, "I am not unaware of the fact that the late Father Walsh visited your office some hours before his death. I thought then it was highly probable that he came to give you the Bibles for safekeeping, or perhaps merely to tell you that he had them and to ask your advice. . . ."

I went to the window and stood looking down into the street. Then, in a low voice and without turning from the window, I said:

"How much?"

"Five thousand."

"I can't hear you."

"Very well. Seventy-five hundred. That is all."

I turned to him.

"I must think it over."

"No. There is no time to think. You must act now."

It was the first time during our interview that the Reverend had displayed any agitation and, although it was nicely controlled, it seemed to me to indicate that there was another group seeking the Bibles with which, he feared, I might be negotiating.

The door-buzzer sounded. Probiloff crossed the room quickly and opened the door. There on the threshold stood an extremely tall and cadaverous individual. His shoulders were wide and bony, and his long black coat was suspended from them in loose folds. He kept his hands thrust deep into the pockets. Definitely, he was something out of a fevered mind.

Probiloff said: Come in, Rauch."

Rauch came in. Probiloff closed the door behind him and turned to me.

"Permit me to introduce my secretary. His name is Rauch. Rauch, this is Mr. D'Arcy."

Rauch nodded his Neanderthal head. A deep guttural bounced about in his enormous chest.

Probiloff said: "Rauch cannot speak a word, Mr. D'Arcy. Unfortunately, his vocal cords were torn from his throat in, ah, an accident he suffered some years ago. . . ."

"Very amusing," I said. "Now that I've seen Repulsive, you may put him back in his cage."

Probiloff nodded, and Rauch withdrew a hand from his overcoat pocket. In it he held a very efficient-looking .38 revolver which he leveled at my head.

"And now, Mr. D'Arcy," Probiloff continued, "Rauch will stand here while you sit quietly in this chair. I am about to take inventory of your apartment."

I slid down into the chair without taking my eyes from the muzzle of the gun. Leaving me in charge of his faithful Rauch, Probiloff proceeded to search the apartment. He went about his work with quick, silent precision. When he had completely exhausted every possible hiding place in the room, he went into my sleeping chamber to continue his search there.

Rauch stood by stoically, the gun exactly two feet from my head. Probiloff returned and stood looking about the room thoughtfully.

"I am not disappointed, Mr. D'Arcy. I really did not think you would be clumsy enough to have the Bibles here. However, there is always the chance that I might prevent some unnecessary expenditure. Now

I am quite ready to talk business."

"And now," I said, "the price has gone up. I want ten thousand."

"Agreed. Ten it is. Where are the Bibles?"

"I shan't be able to deliver them for a few days. But I must insist upon a down payment. Merely to show your good faith, you understand."

Without hesitation, Probiloff reached into the inner pocket of his coat and drew forth a billfold. He counted out ten bills. They were for one hundred dollars each. He threw the money onto my desk.

"I shall make a payment of one thousand dollars. You will be given the balance on delivery of the Bibles." He lowered his voice and his eyes slipped significantly to Rauch. "And, Mr. D'Arcy, you will be showing great wisdom in keeping your promise to deliver. I shall see you again before the week is out." He held forth his gloved hand. "Au revoir. I am sure our association will be mutually profitable."

He shook my hand ceremoniously, turned and nodded to Rauch, who continued to glare at me, and then they left.

I went to the desk and wrote the name of Father Walsh across the face of an envelope. Into this I slid the ten crisp one-hundred-dollar notes.

I remembered that the priest had had a spinster sister who depended upon him to a great extent for her support. She would undoubtedly be able to put this money to good use. I even recalled her name from out of my dim childhood recollections — Catherine.

I placed the envelope in the inner pocket of the suit I would wear. I did not seal it. I had a strong conviction that more money would be added to the sum I had already collected.

I took up the telephone and instructed the hotel operator to ring my office. I could hear the whining ring, then Susan's voice:

"Mr. D'Arcy's office. Good morning."

"This is Mr. D'Arcy."

"I'm sorry, but Mr. D'Arcy is not in. Would you care to leave a message?"

"This *is* D'Arcy, Duchess. I am not calling to speak to myself!"

"Oh, Mr. D'Arcy! I — I . . ."

"Very well, Duchess. Has a woman been in or called on the telephone this morning?"

"No, Mr. D'Arcy. But there was a man here to see you. Just a few minutes ago."

"Did he leave his name?"

"No, sir. He said he would be back later."

"Good. Now, listen closely, Dutchess. You must make a strenuous effort to understand every syllable and do exactly as I say. In my private office, on one of the shelves near the desk, you will find a copy of Oscar Wilde's *Memoirs* and a copy of *Culinary Adventures with Rector*. Wrap them both into a neat package, one that looks like a parcel of books, and meet me in twenty minutes in front of the library on Fifth Avenue. Is that clear?"

"Yes, sir. I understand."

THE DOORMAN held the door open for me as I stepped into the street. I went to the curb and made a very obvious show of looking for a cab. Then I saw him. Rauch had not disappointed me. He was posted across the street in a doorway, exactly as I knew he would be, a newspaper up to his face.

To facilitate matters for him, I waited until two cabs cruised down the street. I stopped the first, entered it, and instructed the driver to take me to Fifth Avenue and Forty-second Street. Behind us was Rauch in the second cab.

My cab drew up to the curb in front of the Public Library. I got out and paid the fare. Rauch's cab slid by slowly, rolled to the corner, and then stopped. His face was still buried behind his newspaper as I turned to look for Susan; and, although I ignored him, I knew that he was watching me from the small window set in the rear of his cab.

Susan was standing near the library steps with the small package under her arm. She looked about anxiously, and her face lit up as she saw me.

I glanced about in what I cansidered to be an obviously furtive manner, and then, apparently satisfied that I had not been followed, I came quickly to the girl. She held out the package.

"I brought the books, Mr. D'Arcy!"

I took the package of books and drew forth from my pocket the envelope in which I had placed Probiloff's money. From the corner of my eye I could see, with great satisfaction, that Rauch was not missing a trick as I extracted one of the bills and held it up in front of Susan.

"This my pet," I said, "is in slight payment for the many insults I have hurled at your bleeding but still unbowed head."

"Oh, Mr. D'Arcy! I don't know what to say!"

"Do you ever?" I murmured. "Just put that bit of pelf into your bag and go right back to the office."

I strode down the cool, high-ceilinged library corridors, my heels making sharp little clicks on the marble floors. Rauch, not very far behind, hugged the wall in a pathetic attempt to make himself inconspicuous, a hopeless task.

My long march through the austere quiet of the spacious halls came to an end at the checkroom. I gave the attendant the package of books. In exchange he offered me a brass tag on which was stamped the number Five.

I dropped the brass check into my pocket, pushed my way through the turnstile, and walked slowly down the steps leading into Forty-second Street. Rauch no longer followed me. He stood in the library corridor, staring stupidly into the checkroom. I could not down a slight feeling of pride when I thought how neatly I had provided Probiloff a problem which would engage his attentions for a bit, remove his watchdog from my trail, and give me time and room in which to breathe.

Susan was speaking into the telephone when I entered my office.

"No," she was saying. "Mr. D'Arcy isn't — oh, one moment, please." She cupped her hand over the transmitter. "A lady wants to talk to you, Mr. D'Arcy."

I walked into my private office and took up the telephone.

"Yes?"

"Mr. D'Arcy?"

I was disappointed. It was not "Rachel."

"Mr. D'Arcy, this is Miss Walsh. Catherine Walsh. Father Walsh's sister. I must see you, Mr. D'Arcy. It's very important."

"And I want to see you, Miss Walsh."

"It's about my brother. He came to see me yesterday. After he had visited you. We had a long talk about — about the trouble. Can I come to your office?"

I said: "No. Don't come to my office. I don't think it would be wise. I live at the Marlin Apartments. Can you be there at four? If I'm not yet in, wait for me in the lobby."

Miss Walsh said: "But I'm afraid to — " She broke off, and then added: "Yes, Mr. D'Arcy. I'll be there."

I put the telephone down slowly. Susan opened the door and looked in.

"Yes, Duchess?"

"That man is here again."

"The one who called this morning?"

"Yes, sir."

"Send him in, Duchess."

Susan withdrew her head, and a moment later my visitor entered. Without preamble, he strode directly to my desk and tossed a calling card down before me.

"Is this your card, sir?"

I glanced down at the card, then raised my eyes to my caller. He was a short, plump little creature in his early fifties, I should say, dressed with neat, tight precision.

"Is that or is that not your card, sir!" he repeated pompously.

"My name is on it."

"Then it *is* your card!" he announced triumphantly.

He took up the card from my desk and pointed it at me as though it were something that crawled.

"Last night you tossed this card into a cab in which a girl was seated. That girl was my daughter. I want to know why you did that!"

I said: "That is my own peculiar method of gaining readers for my column. I also put cards in doorbells, letterboxes, and the men's lavatory in Grand Central Station."

He said: "You asked her to come and talk to you. About some Bibles. I want to know what you meant by that!"

I rose from my chair with startling abruptness and went to the window. I stood with my back to him and stared down into the street. This, I thought, must be the second group, the group which the Reverend Probiloff seemed to fear; and this, of course, was the group of which the girl was a member.

I glanced at the little man from a corner of my eye. Like an indignant pouter pigeon, he had swelled the upper part of his torso until I feared he would burst all over my carpet. I decided there was only one course to pursue with this pixie. I turned to him suddenly, and when I spoke my voice was curt and sharp.

"How dare you come into my office and make demands upon me! Trying to overwhelm me with your nauseating pomposity! Playing the outraged father of the raped virgin! How dare you!"

The little pixie stepped back.

"But, Mr. D'Arcy . . ." he faltered, a shade of white creeping into the pink of his cheeks.

"Stop drooling!" I continued, advancing upon him. "If you've come to talk business, I'll listen."

"You are a violent man, Mr. D'Arcy," he said softly.

"I am a busy man. I've no time for idle chatter."

"Where I come from, Prague, we do not do business that way."

I said: "Unfortunately, you are now doing business in my town. You will either do it my way or not at all."

My anonymous friend bowed his head slightly and stretched his lips into a childlike smile.

"Of course. I must constantly be reminded that I am in Rome. May I sit down?"

I nodded curtly as I lit a cigarette, neglecting to offer him one.

"First, permit me to introduce myself," he began. "My name is Ernst Helms. My native city is Prague. But my work takes me all over the world. I am a dealer in rare books: limited editions, firsts, errata. Wealthy collectors retain me to unearth certain books which they might need to complete a collection. I have been commissioned by a client to find for him two books which he is most anxious to possess. They are, strangely enough, Bibles.

"I finally traced these Bibles to a priest named Father Walsh. I talked with him via telephone, and an appointment was made for last night. My daughter was to examine the Bibles in his possession. Well, sir, she went to keep the appointment last night and — But the rest, of course, you know."

My eyes met those of Mr. Helms squarely, and he dropped his gaze.

"Your daughter lied to me last night," I told him. "I don't like to deal with people I cannot trust."

"Please trust me. I assure you — "

"But your daughter — "

"She is young, inexperienced. Sometimes she is given to — to flights of fancy. But I am old, I am experienced, I am reliable, I am discreet. Yes, that is how I am. You may trust me. Please?"

I pretended to consider his plea as he sat forward anxiously on the edge of his seat.

"Very well. And now you want me to help you track down the Bibles. Is that it?"

Helms said: "No, Mr. D'Arcy, no. Not quite. I want to *buy* them from you."

I said: "Then you've come to the wrong man, Mr. Helms. I am not a bookdealer. I cannot sell you anything. But I am a newspaperman. I might be able to help you *find* something."

Helms settled back in his chair, his eyes once more mere slits. He said: *"Ummmmmmmmm!"*

I said: "Yes. I thought you would understand."

"And — what is your fee?" he asked.

"We will talk fee later. Right now, a — well, call it a retainer."

"Ummmmmmmmmmmm," he repeated, and then added: "How much will you require?"

"As much as the traffic will bear."

Helms started to speak, then checked his words abruptly, stared at me, and in sudden decision took forth his billfold. He started to extract some money, but again he hesitated.

"How do I know you have the Bibles?"

"I did not say I have them."

"Then you know where they are? How do I know you know where they are!"

"You don't know anything," I said.

"How do I know you aren't lying to me!" His voice was now extremely shrill, and there was something repulsively feminine in his hysterical anger. "How do I know you aren't a fake, a fraud!"

"Now, now — you'll get nowhere by flattery," I warned.

"You haven't got the Bibles," he raced on. "You said so yourself! You don't know where they are!"

As he continued, my eyes remained riveted to his face in utter fascination. His cheeks and forehead grew scarlet. The arteries in his temples beat furiously as the blood pounded through his head. He had worked himself up into a choking rage.

"You are a swindler, a thief! Why should I give you any money? You are trying to rob me!"

He was now pounding on my desk with his ridiculous fists. The door opened and Susan put her frightened face into the room.

Without moving my body, without getting up from my chair, and quite without anger, I slapped Helms hard across the mouth. It was a full, stinging blow. He staggered back. I leaped to my feet. I seized his lapels. There was froth at the corners of his mouth. His eyes were rolling wildly. I could see nothing but the whites. I held both lapels knotted tightly in one fist, and with my free hand I slapped him again and again.

"Quick! Susan! Get water!"

She withdrew her head quickly.

With all my strength, I slapped Helms again. He opened his mouth. I was not quick enough. He caught my wrist between his teeth and sank them viciously into my flesh. I screamed with the pain.

Susan ran in with a tumbler of water. She dashed it full into Helm's face. He opened his mouth to gasp, and I sent my fist crashing against his jaw. He slumped to the floor at my feet.

My wrist was badly lacerated. The blood ran down my fingers onto the floor, some onto my right shoe. I took a bottle of whisky from the cabinet, removed the cork with my teeth, put the neck of the bottle to my lips, and drank in great gulps. The rest I poured over the laceration.

I bent to the unconscious Helms, lifted him like a babe, and dumped him unceremoniously onto the couch. Quickly I removed his coat, loosened his tie, and tore a wide strip out the back of his shirt. I gave this to the quaking Susan. With fumbling fingers she bandaged my wrist. Neither of us spoke.

I turned to look at Helms. He was still unconscious. I removed his billfold from his coat and riffled through it. I found no means of identification, none at all, but the leather bore the stamp of a San Francisco dealer. The wallet contained nothing but twelve hundred dollars in cash. I put one thousand dollars on my desk and returned the balance to the billfold. I went through Helms's clothing thoroughly, and found a letter addressed to him. It was a brief note written on the stationery of one Serko Hodakis, a lawyer with offices in New York City, and it had been sent to Ernst Helms, Esq., Hotel Ambassador, East Chicago, Ill.

DEAR ERNST,
I am enclosing the draft of twenty-five hundred dollars which you demand. Please be extremely careful how you use the money. I do wish you would see fit to give me more of your confidence. After so many years, I do not mind saying that your attitude now is both puzzling and painful. Surely, I have always proved myself a friend.
Affectionately,

And it was signed by Mr. Hodakis.

Suddenly Helms moaned, jerked his head from side to side erratically, and sat up with startling abruptness. He blinked his eyes, looked about in great bewilderment. I replaced the letter, dropped the coat I had been searching, and went to his side.

As I crossed the room, I told Susan to wait outside. She went quickly. I stood over Helms, and he looked up at me questioningly. "What — ?"

"You're all right now."

He rose to his feet unsteadily.

"What happened?"

"You were slightly ill."

I helped the dazed man into his coat, fixed his tie.

His hand went to his inner pocket to feel for his billfold. I took it up from my desk. He tore it from my fingers, opened it hastily, then looked up at me in fright.

"My money! Where is my money! Please!"

I took the bills from the desk and gave them to him. I said: "You have one thousand dollars there. That is what I want as a retainer to help you find the Bibles. ... The Bibles marked *E. B.*"

Helms had begun to insert the sheaf of bills into his wallet, but when I mentioned the initials *E. B.*, he hesitated, the money still in his hand. I sensed his indecisive moment, took the money from his fingers, and put it in my desk. He offered no objection.

"How soon will you deliver the books?" he asked.

"In a few days," I said.

Helms considered for a moment. "Very well," he agreed.

"Where can I reach you?"

"No. I will come back here. Three days?"

I said I had been delighted to meet him and would expect him in three days, and he turned quietly and left the office.

I BENT OVER the low basin behind the screen and scrubbed my hands thoroughly, removing all traces of the blood which had poured from my wrist. Then with a damp cloth I did a fairly effective temporary job of removing the stains from the cuff of my trousers and from my shoe.

The door opened a trifle and Susan looked in.

"Your — your friend was very excited. . . ."

"Think nothing of it, Susan. He was simply overwhelmed at making my acquaintance."

"Oh."

There was a pause.

"Susan, take this," I said suddenly, putting a bill on the desk. "Dash around the corner to McCall's Bookshop. Buy a Bible. Quickly."

"A — Bible?"

"Don't stare at me as though I were in my second dotage, child, but go!"

Susan went.

I opened the drawer in which I had placed the money taken from Ernst Helms, added it to Probiloff's in the envelope marked "Father Walsh," and then put the envelope back into my pocket.

I took up the telephone and dialed a number, and after a brief wait a voice on the other end announced:

"Central Taxi Service."

I said: "Carl? This is D'Arcy of the *Post*. Last night one of your decrepit hacks picked up a girl in front of Bianca's on Ramm Street. About ten, I should think. I'd like to know where he took her."

Carl said: "Hold on. I'll look at the sheets." A moment, and then: "Here it is: A dollar-fifteen run to the Hotel Bolton on Central Park South."

I said: "Thank you, pet. If ever you'd like someone's reputation annihilated, just point him out."

I put the telephone away, consulted the directory, found the number I was seeking, and again spun the dial. A man's nasal voice answered:

"Bishop Martin's residence."

"Is Bishop Martin at home?"

He was, and after some colloquy I made an appointment with him for two in the afternoon.

I put the telephone aside. I glanced at my watch, and it read five minutes before noon.

Susan returned with a Bible under her arm.

"Here is the Bible, Mr. D'Arcy."

"Excellent, Duchess. Now, you may sit in that chair and place the Bible on your lap."

Susan, now quite beyond wonder, did as I instructed.

"Like this, Mr. D'Arcy?"

"Like that, Duchess," I said gravely. I rose to my feet and slowly paced the floor as I spoke: "Tell me, my sweet, what do you know about the Walls of Jericho?"

Susan stared at me blankly.

"The — Walls of Jericho?"

"Precisely. You've heard of them, no doubt?"

"Oh, of course, sir! It — they . . . well, it's in the story about Joshua. That's it, sir. Joshua!"

"Joshua," I said approvingly. "Excellent. Now, I suggest that you turn to this man Joshua in the

Bible there on your lap, and read to me the story of the Walls of Jericho."

With a deal of fumbling, and with one eye on the alert to see if I had not suddenly taken leave of my senses, Susan finally found the chapter in the Bible dealing with Jericho. She cleared her throat self-consciously and began to read in a timid voice:

"Chapter six: 'Now Jericho was straitly shut up, because of . . .' " She broke off and looked up at me: "Is that what you want, Mr. D'Arcy?" I nodded, and she went on:

". . . up, because of the children of Israel: none went out and none came in.

"And the Lord said unto Joshua, See, I have given unto thine hand Jericho, and the kind thereof, and the mighty men of valor.

"And ye shall compass the city, all ye men of war, and go round about the city once. Thus shalt thou do six days.

"And seven priests shall bear before the ark seven trumpets of rams' horns: and the seventh day ye shall compass the city seven times, and the priests shall blow with the trumpets.

"And it shall come to pass, that when they make a long blast with the ram's horn, and when ye hear the sound of the trumpet, all the people shall shout with a great shout: and the wall of the city shall fall down flat, and the people shall ascend up, every man straight before him.

"And Joshua the son of Nun called the priests, and said unto them . . ."

"That will do, Duchess."

I rose wearily, crossed to the window and stared moodily into the street.

"The Priests and the Rams' Horns and the Walls Came Tumbling Down," I murmured. "What do you think, Duchess?"

"Well, I — That's what it says in the Bible, sir."

I sighed deeply, took my hat, placed it carefully on my head, and went to the door.

"Will you be back this afternoon, Mr. D'Arcy?"

"I don't know, Duchess," I said. "If anyone calls, you may say that I am at my tailor being fitted for a new strait jacket. Something simple in rhinestones."

I opened the door.

"And — what shall I do with the Bible, sir?"

"Make a brief synopsis and leave it on my desk."

I closed the door behind me.

My cab drew up before Marco's Book Shop on Fifty-ninth Street between Park and Lexington Avenues. I descended the three steps from the sidewalk which led into the establishment, and stopped for a moment inside the threshold as I attempted to adjust my eyes to the sudden gloom.

Marco's was a tiny square cubbyhole filled with used books, old papers, and heavy dust; but it was well known to collectors of rare items.

As I stood in Marco's doorway, a voice called out from the dark:

"You want to buy or just look?"

I blinked rapidly two or three times, and was finally able to distinguish the vague outlines of Marco seated behind his desk in the rear of the shop. As I went to him, he reminded me of nothing but an oversized, bald-headed mole glaring with belligerence at a carrier of light.

I said: "I come neither to buy or look. I come seeking knowledge. May I advance?"

Marco's voice softened to a mere truculence.

"Oh, it is you, D'Arcy."

"Indeed, it is. I want only a little information, Marco. Nothing but a little information."

Marco relaxed and his face brightened.

"So? Information? About books?"

"About books. And I might have a customer for you."

He said: "Good, good. I will give you a commission," and then added hastily: "A small commission. Who is it?"

"A wealthy friend of mine," I said, "is thinking of enlarging his collection of rare books."

Marco asked: "What kind of books?"

I said: "Bibles."

There was a pause. Marco sat very still and looked up at me without speaking. Then:

"Bibles?" he echoed.

I said: "Yes. Rare Bibles. He would like to purchase a few items. Price is no consideration."

Marco looked up sharply, and when he spoke his voice was curt. "I've been in this business for forty years. Maybe once every ten years somebody will ask about such an item. And now . . ."

"And now what?"

He waved a hand carelessly.

"It doesn't matter. . . . Well, D'Arcy, of course there are all categories of rare Bibles: firsts, association copies, errata, and so forth. It all depends on what your friend is looking for and how much he is willing to spend."

"He is extremely wealthy . . ."

"There are certain items he can pick up for, say, fifty dollars; and others," he added casually, "that would cost him up to a half a million dollars."

"Half a million dollars!"

Marco nodded.

"Of course, there are only perhaps a few such items known, and they are in the possession of museums and governments. But that's just to give you an idea of the price range. Now, how much do you think this friend of yours will spend?"

I said: "I really don't know, Marco. If you will give me an idea of what might be available, I'll talk to him about it."

Marco leaned back in his chair, laced his fingers behind his head, and closed his eyes.

"There is a nice little item," he began, "that I could put my hands on for about eight thousand, more or less, and guarantee delivery and authenticity. It is the Pentateuch in Hebrew with the Greater Massorah in the upper and lower margins, and the Lesser Massorah at the side.

"I can also," he continued smoothly, "make an effort to buy the so-called *Wicked Bible*. There are only four copies extant, and it would cost at least thirty to forty thousand. An edition of several thousand was printed by Robert Barker in London in 16 — *ummm*, yes, 1631. But because of a typographical error, the King ordered the entire issue destroyed and the printer was fined 300 pounds. Only four of the books were saved. The error appears in the seventh commandment, and in the *Wicked Bible* it reads: 'Thou shalt commit adultery.' Barker dropped the *not*."

Marco permitted one eye to open, through which he

glared at me.

"Well?"

"I don't know," I replied slowly, and then casually added: "Do you know of anything that deals with one book in particular: the Book of Joshua?"

I could almost hear Marco's other eye fly open. He stared at me like a startled owl.

"Joshua," he said softly. "Yes . . . There is the Pentateuch and Book of Joshua." He paused. "Did you ever hear of the Pentateuch and Book of Joshua, the Aelfric Book?" I did not speak, but shook my head negatively. "Yes," he went on, "It was made in the eleventh century by Aelfric the Grammarian, Abbott of Cerne and Eynsham. Yes. There are only two copies of it in existence. And they are priceless . . ."

I could feel the muscles in my stomach slowly tighten.

I asked: "Do you know what they would cost?"

Marco said: "More money than your friend has."

"What do you mean?"

"They cannot be bought."

"They cannot be bought?"

"They belong to the British Museum."

"In London?"

"In London."

"But — they can be seen?"

"Not until after the war."

"Why not?"

"Packed away. In vaults."

"Because of the bombings?"

"In electrically locked vaults."

"And they will be brought out? After the war?"

"If they are still there."

"Ah?"

Marco shrugged.

"Bombings, fire — who knows?"

"It — they wouldn't be easy to buy — or sell?"

Marco's voice dropped to a faint whisper.

"One or two collectors. They would buy. They would pay. Very high. Just to possess. Just for the pleasure. In secret. They would pay. Very high."

Marco continued to gaze at me from beneath his

heavy-hanging, red-rimmed lids. I rose to my feet. My mind was whirling.

I said: "Thank you, Marco. You . . . you've been a great help."

We went to the door.

I said: "I will speak to my friend. If he wants to buy anything, I will let you know."

Marco said: "Thank you. I also *buy* books, you know," and then added hastily: "if he has anything to sell, I mean."

Marco held my eyes for a moment, then I said goodby and started up the steps, but before I could gain the street the bookdealer called my name and I turned to look down upon him standing in the basement.

I said: "Yes, Marco?"

For the briefest instant Marco hesitated. Then, with the incongruous gesture of raising his arm and pointing a meaningless finger at me, he said:

"I just remembered. Strange coincidence. Two days ago a man was in here. He, too, asked about the Aelfric Book of Joshua. I think he was a friend of yours. Anyway, the newspapers said you found his body."

I opened my mouth to speak, but no words came forth. For the first time in my life, I did not know what to say. I think I grinned foolishly and Marco grinned back, and then I turned away and went into the street and got into a waiting cab and drove off.

Chapter Three

T HE LOBBY of the Hotel Bolton was hot and humid and almost completely deserted. A few transients sat about with unread newspapers on their laps, chins boring into their chests, and fast asleep.

Leaning with one elbow on the cigar counter, the ever-present toothpick in his lips, was Tiny Stover, the house detective. I wandered up behind him and whispered over his shoulder:

"Buy some French postcards, pal?"

Stover swung about to face me.

"Ha! Comedian!" He shifted the toothpick to the other side of his mouth. "What's new?"

"I have come to ask a favor, Tiny."

"Sure. What's the name?"

"Helms. Ernst Helms. And daughter."

Stover led me into the office, and he drew forth the card file of registrations. He flipped the cards over rapidly as he called the names:

"*Ummm* . . . let's see . . . Hebble, Hedwig, Herbert . . ." He looked up as he slid the drawer shut with a snap. "Sorry, my friend, no Helms."

"Thank you Tiny. My faith is justified. I did not think he would live in a house of shame." I pressed a bill into his hand.

I looked at my watch and noted that I still had a half-hour before my appointment with Bishop Martin fell due. I recalled that I had not had any food that morning and the thought shocked me.

I went into the dining room and started for a table, but halted abruptly when I saw "Rachel."

A waiter was serving a plate of soup, and she appeared to be quite alone. I drifted over to her table and without a word sat in the chair opposite her. She looked up, spoon poised in midair. For an instant the blood drained from her cheeks, but she recovered quickly. I nodded and smiled pleasantly.

I said: "You're looking extremely charming this afternoon. I simply called to return something you left with me last night."

I leaned across the small table and kissed her on the lips. Her eyes narrowed as she drew her head back.

"All right. You've returned it. Now what else do you want?"

"Food." I turned to the waiter. "Very dry double Martini with onion, sea food Newburgh, double order escalloped potatoes, string beans, squash, five slices of buttered rye bread toast, coffee." The waiter nodded, glided away. I looked up at the girl and smiled. "I am a growing boy. Your soup is getting cold."

She leaned back in her chair, and there was a small amused smile on her lips. She regarded me for a moment through half-closed eyes.

"I am in no mood for a merry-go-round," she said curtly. "Why did you come here?"

"For two reasons: one, I like their waiters; two, I have some news for you. It might prove quite a shock. You had better prepare yourself for it."

"Please don't play cute! I can't stand cuteness in a man weighing more than two hundred pounds!"

"Very well," I sighed. "You've attacked my ego at its most vulnerable point. I shall no longer be considerate but will tell you straight off. Your father, my child, was not beheaded in Harbin. Or was it Peiping? He bribed his jailer with a tin of slightly used chewing tobacco which he had been hoarding for just such an emergency."

"So he got away!"

"A very clever man."

"And when did you learn all this about my father?"

"Hasn't he told you? Oh, dear!" I exclaimed, simulating chagrin. "What have I done? Was it meant to be a surprise? Yes. He came this morning to my office to say hello. Told me he intends to make a new life for himself, even a new name. Fothersgill-Fortescue, said he, died in China, and Ernst Helms was born. He was very charming. He said 'hello' and I said 'hello' and it was all very delightful, and then he suddenly became quite ill. . . ."

The girl leaned forward, concern in her eyes.

"He became ill?"

I waved her alarm aside. "Oh, nothing really serious. Nothing that a year or two in any first-rate sanitarium would not cure. But I don't believe he should be permitted to wander about the city by himself. The way he is, I mean."

The waiter approached with the sea food Newburgh, the escalloped potatoes, the string beans and the squash, the buttered toast and the coffee. The girl settled back in her chair, ignoring the food the waiter placed before her, never taking her eyes from my face.

I poured the coffee, sprinkled salt and pepper on the food, took up a fork, and started to eat.

"They've burned the potatoes," I sighed. "They never fail." I ate in silence, enjoying the food. Then I said: "You may go ahead. I don't mind conversation while I eat. You may start talking."

"About what?"

"Simply that rare and delicate thing known to some as the Truth. About you, your father, the Bibles."

The girl hesitated, then her mouth relaxed into a small smile.

"You say you spoke with my father this morning. What did *he* tell you?"

"The rambling story which he and you dreamed up, and I found it all very dull and unimaginative."

"Then I am sure you would find the truth even duller."

"Coming from your lips," I said, "nothing could be dull."

"Take A for effort," she said dryly. "But if you have something my father wants to buy, why not sell it to him and let it go at that?"

"Because I am waiting to hear from another bidder."

"Who?" she asked quickly.

"The British Museum."

I sipped my coffee and she sat very still. An excellent actress, I thought, noting the expression óf blank puzzlement on her face.

"The British Museum?" she echoed.

"Precisely."

I sat back and poured more coffee into my cup. There was silence while the girl struggled to come to a decision. Then she began:

"Mr. D'Arcy, I —"

"Go on, my dear."

"I'm confused. I mean, I don't know any more if ..."

"Yes?"

She hesitated, then looked up at me slowly. Her eyes were distressed.

"Can I really trust you?" she asked.

"What do you expect me to say? There seems to be a naïve strain running through the Helms line. This morning your father asked me the same question. I've learned through disillusioning experience, my dear, that when anyone asks me if I can really be trusted, it's the last thing they intend to do. What name are you registered under?"

"All right," she said abruptly, ignoring my questtion. "Perhaps I'm trying to be too clever. But before I say anything, you'll have to answer one thing. Have you got the Bibles?"

"You haven't told me what name you're registered under."

Abruptly her face grew rebellious.

"Why should I? You come poking about like a tomcat in an alley, making demands and asking a million questions in your nauseating, patronizing manner, expecting people to confide in you while you sit back smugly with your lips tight! Why should I answer you!"

During her tirade, I looked up over the girl's shoulder and was shocked when I saw two men approaching from the lobby in earnest conversation. One was Mr. Ernst Helms. The other was Marco.

The girl's flow of words continued, and I rose abruptly to my feet. I did not want to confront Helms and Marco without time to think. I tossed a bill down on the table and interrupted the girl curtly.

"Very well! I've no time to listen to a lot of fishwife bilge!"

I turned and hurriedly left the restaurant through the street entrance.

In a corner cigar store I found a telephone booth. I deposited a coin in the slot and dialed the long distance operator. I told her that I was D'Arcy of the *Morning Post* and living at the Marlin Apartments and that I wanted to speak with John Barrett at the San Francisco *Ledger,* a newspaper in San Francisco, and that the call was to be charged to my account at the Marlin. The operator said very well and she would call me back in a few minutes. In a surprisingly short while the connection was made.

Barrett's voice came over the wire: "D'Arcy! How are you, you lecher."

"Superb. And how is Prince Revolting?"

"I'm more beautiful than ever. Why the sudden call, feller?"

"John, I want a favor."

"Of course you do. And by the by, what is the mad meaning of that surrealist drawing that just came in the noon mail?"

"Do you recognize her?"

"Well, I have it here before me and, when I turn it upside down, it looks suspiciously like—"

"Listen. I could not think of her name last night, but I've just been with her again, and I'm fairly certain I know it now: Patricia Behrens. I want as much information about her as you can gather within the next few hours. Wire it immediately to my apartment at the Marlin."

"You shall have it before day is done."

"It's extremely important, John."

"When the old master speaks in those tones, I can only say: 'Rely on me.' "

I put the receiver back in its place and left the cigar store to keep my appointment with Bishop Martin.

An oldish young man with jet-black hair, high celluloid collar, and squeaking patent-leather shoes, stood on the threshold of Bishop Martin's reception room and signaled silently for me to follow.

He led me down a long, narrow corridor, up a short flight of steps which seemed to twist back upon itself three times, then halted before a wide oak door on the first landing. He tapped his knuckles on the door very softly and, without waiting for a response, threw it open.

Set at an angle at the farthermost corner of the huge, high-ceilinged room was a massive mahogany desk which dwarfed the rest of the room's furnishings into insignificance. Behind it sat Bishop Martin. He nodded almost imperceptibly, gesturing for me to approach, a wintry smile on his thin lips.

"You are Mr. D'Arcy?" he asked. I confessed that I was, and he nodded his head in agreement. "Yes, I do remember you now. You were with Captain Griffin at Father Walsh's residence last night."

"Yes. And it is because of Father Walsh that I am here."

"Please go on."

I hesitated for an instant, trying to frame my request, then decided to put it point-blank.

"I want your permission to examine Father Walsh's effects: his papers, books — and so forth."

"Why?"

"Because I am convinced that he was murdered."

For a long moment there was a frigid silence. The Bishop's face remained impassive. Finally he said:

"And — just what leads you to believe he was murdered?"

"I have excellent reason."

"What is it?"

"I — I'd rather not discuss my reasons just yet."

The Bishop tapped a delicate finger against his chin. His shrewd eyes probed my face.

"Mr. D'Arcy, I am going to ask you to listen carefully to what I have to say."

He spoke in slow cadence, as though carefully choosing his words.

"All of Father Walsh's associates have been profoundly shocked by the tragedy which has befallen him. It has been a great strain, and our efforts to protect his memory have been respected to a great degree by both the police and the press."

He hesitated, then turned to look at me. His voice was low and charged with great sincerity.

"If I thought for one single moment that there might be the slightest truth in your theory, you would have my fullest cooperation. Father Walsh was good and kind and understanding. He led a beautiful life' of service. He did not have an enemy in the world. And that is why I am convinced that you are wrong. There was no one in this world who could wish him harm. And despite the strong temptation — yes, I will admit it *is* a temptation — to believe that he was murdered rather than a suicide, I cannot in all conscience do so. . . . I — That is all, Mr. D'Arcy."

He turned back to the window in dismissal.

I went to the door, opened it, and then turned back to the Bishop.

"I have one favor to ask of you," I said. He looked up slowly. "I'd rather the police knew nothing of our conversation this afternoon."

He nodded without speaking.

I closed the door softly behind me, walked down the twisting steps, and out into the street.

ONE HOUR LATER I was in the gymnasium at my club, sparring a few rounds with René, when the page told me that I was wanted on the telephone. I had had some open time before my appointment with Catherine Walsh, and, after leaving Bishop Martin, I had decided to spend an hour in a brief workout.

I threw my robe about my shoulders, leaped over the ropes of the ring, and went to the telephone booths.

"This is D'Arcy," I said into the wire.

I could hear the club's switchboard operator shifting her telephone lines, and then Susan's voice came over the wire.

"Mr. D'Arcy?"

"What is it, Susan?"

"Oh, Mr. D'Arcy, I've been trying to get you all over. Mr. Hodakis called. Three times. It's very important. That's what he said."

I asked: "Mr. — who?"

Susan said: "Hodakis. Serko Hodakis."

I said: "I don't believe it. No one could possibly be named Serko Hodakis."

Şusan said: "That's what he said, Mr. D'Arcy. Very important, and you're to call his office right away. Columbus 9-3320, and it's about Mr. Helms. He said to be sure to tell you that."

"About Mr. Helms?"

"That's what he said, Mr. D'Arcy."

I recalled the note I had found in Helms's coat, then said:

"Very well, Duchess."

I gave the operator the telephone number of Mr. Serko Hodakis. After a short wait a singsong voice said:

"Serko Hodakis. G'Afternoon."

I said: "This is Mr. D'Arcy calling Mr. Hodakis."

The voice said: "Oh, One moment, please."

Another brief pause, and a man's booming voice rumbled across the wires:

"Hello, there, Mr. D'Arcy. This is Hodakis."

He sounded like the cheer leader at a pep convention of insurance salesmen.

I said firmly: "My secretary reported that you have been calling my office."

He said: "Yes! Yes, indeed! Would like to see you this afternoon. Right now, if possible. Eh?"

I said: "I am at my club, Mr. Hodakis. Perhaps if you tell me what — ?"

He said: "Yes, yes, sorry! Want to talk to you about Helms. Ernst Helms. You know him, eh?"

"Ernst Helms?" I said cautiously.

"Quite all right, Mr. D'Arcy. Yes, indeed! All in the strictest confidence. I am his attorney. Looking after his interests, so to speak. Shall we meet at your club? Don't mind a bit!"

"Very well, Mr. Hodakis. I haven't much time to spare, but if your business is brief, I'll come to your office."

Hodakis said: "Splendid, splendid! I'm in 30 Rockefeller Plaza. Forty-fourth floor. Hodakis and

Spiridon. Spiridon is dead. How soon can you be here?"

I said: "My condolences to Mrs. Spiridon. I'll leave my club in about twenty minutes."

"Then you won't be here for almost an hour, eh?"

"More or less."

Hodakis said: "Excellent, excellent! That will give me time to dispose of a small matter I have on hand and then we shall meet. Good-by, good-by, thank you!"

The frosted glass of the door on the forty-fourth floor of the R. C. A. Building bore the legend:

HODAKIS & SPIRIDON
Attorneys-at-Law

Spiridon is dead, I thought idiotically as I opened the door and entered the reception room. A girl at a switchboard peeked through a cubbyhole.

"Yes?"

I said: "I'd like to see Mr. Spiridon."

"I'm sorry, but Mr. Spir —" She broke off abruptly and stared up at me through bulging eyes. "But Mr. Spiridon is dead a year!" she exclaimed.

"Really?"

"He died when he was shot in a hold-up!"

"The wages of sin," I murmured. "Is Mr. Hodakis alive? If he is, please tell him Mr. D'Arcy is here. If not, I won't wait."

The girl looked at me uncertainly.

"I'm sorry, sir, but Mr. Hodakis was not expecting you so soon. He said if you came in to tell you—I mean, he was suddenly called over to Magistrate's Court, but he will only be a few minutes. He would like to have you wait for him."

I do not know how long I sat glancing through the newspapers, but finally the door opened and a man entered. I knew at once that this was Mr. Serko Hodakis himself.

Mr. Hodakis was very much the bluff type: hale, hearty, and large in every dimension. He had an enormous and extremely handsome head covered by a thick shock of wavy stone-gray hair, and shoulders almost as broad as the door. Under his arm, he carried a bulging portfolio.

"Mr. D'Arcy?"

I rose to my feet. He closed his fingers about my hand and, although I am no small man myself, my hand was lost to view.

"Yes. Mr. Hodakis?"

The large features of his face melted into an ugly but not unpleasant smile. He pumped my arm with a great deal of enthusiasm.

"Waiting long? Terribly sorry. Didn't think you'd get here so soon. You understand. Eh?" and then to the girl at the switchboard: "Any calls for me, Miss Ruvetli?" Without waiting for her negative response he turned back to me and continued his flow of apologies as he led me into his private office and closed the door behind us.

"Mr. D'Arcy," he began, "I know that you are a very busy man — yes, indeed! — so I shall be brief and come right to the point: I've called you to ask your help in behalf of Ernst Helms, my client. Know who you are, your reputation, and am sure that when I tell you what it is that's troubling me, you will be glad to give me your help. Eh?"

I said: "If I can."

He said: "There! I knew you would. Yes, indeed! This morning Mr. Helms visited your office. Eh?"

I hesitated slightly, then asked:

"How do you know that Mr. Helms visited my office this morning?"

"He told me so." Hodakis left the window, went to his desk, and took from a drawer a long, narrow ledger. He flipped the pages, found what he wanted, and looked up to me. "Look at this a moment, eh?"

I went to the desk and glanced down at the ledger page. Across the top, in an even, Spencerian hand, was written: *Acc't Ernst Helms.* My eye ran down a column of figures which, of course, I did not understand, and came to rest on an entry under which Hodakis held his finger. The entry read: *8/24 pd. to D'Arcy $1,000.*

Hodakis said: "Yes, Mr. D'Arcy. Mr. Helms told me that he gave you that money and asked me to enter it in the records of his account."

I looked up slowly. "Mr. Helms, you say, told you that he gave me one thousand dollars. Did Mr. Helms show you a receipt for that money?"

Hodakis waved an impatient hand. "I am not greatly concerned with whether or not he did give you that money, Mr. D'Arcy. No, indeed. That is only a drop in the bucket — in the ocean, I might say. Mr. Helms has paid out thousands and thousands. Oh, yes, indeed! You can believe that. This has been going on for quite some time, in cities all over the country — and many foreign places, too. But this is the first time, this is actually the first time, I've ever been able to find and talk to anyone to whom he was supposed to have given any money. That is the reason, Mr. D'Arcy; yes, that is why I called you."

I said: "I'm afraid, Mr. Hodakis, that you have not made yourself very clear; at least, not to me. From what you have told me, all I can gather is that your client does not wish to confide this particular business in you. I still don't understand what you want of me."

Hodakis did not answer immediately. He simply looked into my face, his eyes grave. Then he closed the ledger on his desk with a small snap, and when he spoke his voice was low and portentous.

"Only this: I want you to tell me exactly *why* Mr. Helms gave you that money — or, if he did not give you any, why he came to see you and what he wanted . . ." As I did not speak, he continued:

"Mr. Helms is a dealer in rare books. His work sometimes takes him on long journeys. The expenses incurred on these trips are usually met by the client for whom he may be working, searching out some item.

"I am his attorney. I handle, and always have handled, all of his finances. He is not a very shrewd businessman, Mr. Helms, and for a long time now he has been drawing large sums of cash through me. Always cash.

"I don't know what he is doing with his money. I admit that he refuses to tell me. I don't know what he is after. All I know is that whatever it is, this search upon which he has embarked is not only draining his fortune, but, more important, is ruining his health.

48

"I am afraid that he is in the hands of a group of ruthless people who are exploiting him. I want to help him. But I can't. He won't let me. But I am terribly worried about him, and it is my duty to help him despite himself.

"And that is why I called you, why I want you to tell me what he said to you, what he wanted of you, why he gave you — or offered to give you — this money."

Throughout the lengthy narrative, Hodakis never once removed his eyes from my face, and when he had finished we both sat quite still as he waited for me to speak; but I remained silent — and for a very good reason: I simply did not know what to say.

What Hodakis had told me certainly made for logic and fitted in nicely with what I had already learned: Ernst Helms was making a determined effort to secure the stolen Aelfric Book of Joshua. This, of course, he could not confide to any ethical lawyer, and it reasonably explained his silence. Hence his sudden demands upon Hodakis for funds without explanation.

But the lawyer, apparently, had placed me in the same unsavory category with all the rest who had taken money from Helms. Hodakis was firmly convinced that in some manner his client was being fleeced, and the entry in the ledger read that I had now joined that charming circle of swindlers who were plucking Helms clean.

The more my mind probed, the more confused did my thoughts become, and I felt that I was getting beyond my depth. I decided that there was only one sure and sane thing for me to do at the moment: Leave Mr. Serko Hodakis as quickly as possible and say as little as possible.

I rose to my feet.

I said: "Yes. Mr. Helms did visit me this morning. And he did give me one thousand dollars."

"Yes? And what did you give him for it?"

"Advice."

Hodakis drew his bushy brows together, making a continuous line of bristle above the deep furrows in the ridge of his nose.

"Advice? On what?"

"On publicity and public relations."

Hodakis rose slowly from his chair, his eyes mere slits and fastened to my face.

"What are you talking about?"

"I am a newspaperman. I know the subject thoroughly. Mr. Helms came to me to tell me that he intends to organize a vast network of circulating libraries. He sought my advice on how to publicize them efficiently. I gave him that advice, and for that I charged him one thousand dollars. That is all. And now, if you will excuse me, I must be going."

I nodded and started for the door.

"One moment!"

Hodakis's voice was sharp and threatening. He came quickly from behind the desk and confronted me. His face was now deeply clouded.

"Yes?"

Hodakis said: "Do you expect me to believe that?"

"No."

"Do you think you can make a fool of me?"

"Yes."

"Well, by God, you can't! You and your whole gang! You've been swindling Helms, by God! And you tell me right now what you gave him for that money, if you gave him *anything,* or I'll call the District Attorney — by God, I will! — and you'll explain to him!"

"Very well," I said. "I was reluctant to tell you anything simply because Helms himself has not seen fit to confide in you."

"You still do not have to tell me anything," said the lawyer. "If your dealings with my client are ethical and can stand a police scrutiny, you need only say you refuse to talk to me and would prefer to explain to the District Attorney."

Mr. Hodakis was certainly exploiting every advantage as he gently rubbed in the salt and waited for me to squirm.

"I think we both are being unnecessarily childish," I said lamely. "I surely have nothing to hide. However, if you fear that in some manner your client is being swindled, I will tell you exactly for what it is that he is negotiating with me: He came to me to help him find a pair of rare books for one of his customers. That is all."

"No, Mr. D'Arcy. That is not all. It is not as simple as all that. You took one thousand dollars from him. I want to know what you gave him for that money."

By now, I was morally certain that Serko Hodakis would not hesitate to involve me with the police if he were not satisfied with my answers, and that was one thing I was determined to avoid at all costs.

I said: "Very well. If you insist. The money which I took from Ernst Helms was in payment for one of the books."

Hodakis opened his mouth to speak, then brought his lips together with a small sound, as though he could not find the question.

"Is there anything else?" I asked.

The lawyer turned to me slowly. His face was grimmer than I had yet seen it, and his hands were tightly clenched behind his back.

"You are telling me the truth," he said.

It was not a question.

"I am telling you the truth."

"Ernst Helms gave you one thousand dollars and you gave him one of two books for which he is searching."

Again it was not a question, but a statement phrased in the legal manner so dear to the ears of judges, juries, and dictaphones. Whatever the lawyer's purpose, it was too late for me to retreat.

I said: "That is correct."

Mr. Hodakis continued to stare at me in stony silence, then took a step toward me. His face was now very close to mine. His eyes bored into me threateningly, and when he spoke, his low voice matched the mood of his eyes.

"Remember, Mr. D'Arcy: it will be a simple matter for me to learn whether or not you *are* telling me the truth. If I find that you have lied, I promise it will go very hard with you. Is that clear?"

"Indeed, it is. You have an unpleasant habit of making yourself disgustingly clear. And now, if you will excuse me — and even if you won't . . ."

I brushed him casually from my path, opened the door, and left his office.

I WAS VERY LATE. My watch read ten minutes before five o'clock when I entered the lobby of my hotel. I looked about the small room, but Catherine Walsh was not there. I went to the desk and was forced to rap for the attention of the clerk, who had suddenly busied himself with some papers in the inner office.

He came out slowly, his eyes glued to the sheets which he rustled in his thin hands.

"Yes, Mr. D'Arcy?"

He did not look up. Apparently, he found the columns of interminable figures utterly fascinating.

"Is there a telegram for me?"

"No, Mr. D'Arcy."

"Was there a lady here to see me?"

"A — No, Mr. D'Arcy."

He rustled a sheet nervously from midpile and gave it his undivided attention with peculiar singleness of purpose.

"Are you ill, Raymond?"

"I — No, Mr. D'Arcy."

He glanced at me briefly without lifting his face from the papers in his hands.

I entered the self-service elevator, punched the proper button, and the cage whisked me up to the seventh floor.

Undoubtedly, I thought, Catherine Walsh had wearied of waiting for me, and I could not blame her. I would make an effort to locate her at once, I decided, as I walked down the hall to my apartment.

I inserted my key in the lock, entered the foyer of my apartment, and closed the door behind me.

"Come right in. Just in time for tea."

I stopped on the threshold of the living room.

"Well, well," I said. "Very gala."

Standing in the center of the room, his hands thrust deep into his ill-kempt trousers, was Captain Frederick Griffin.

Slumped down at his complete ease, in a large chair, his feet slung over the arm, was Detective Lucas. He grinned briefly in greeting.

Standing at the window, staring moodily into the street, was dour-faced Detective Regan. He turned his head to me as I entered, nodded slightly, then returned his gaze to the street below.

I noticed that the room had been thoroughly searched. My bookshelves, my desk — all in a state of confusion. I was furious at this high-handed procedure, and I turned to Griffin coldly.

But a certain glint in his eye made me feel apprehensive. I began to sense real trouble. "Why did you come here?" I asked.

Griffin stared at me grimly.

He turned and went abruptly to my bedroom door and threw it open. "You got a visitor waiting inside."

I hesitated and looked at the men.

Regan nodded and grinned a humorless grin.

Lucas shook his head despairingly. "Ah, D'Arcy," he sighed. "You're a bad boy. A real problem child, I might say."

I walked to the threshold of the bedroom and looked in. I could see no one. I turned to Griffin.

He said: "Go on in. Make yourself at home."

I took three small, reluctant steps into the darkling room, and then halted abruptly. I had seen it. It was lying on the floor on the other side of my bed and near the small table on which stood my telephone.

It was the body of an old woman. I can't remember what she was wearing. All I can see now is that she was very frail, very dainty, and very small. She was lying on her back, her right arm twisted grotesquely under her. Her left arm was flung out rigidly across the carpet, the fingers on her childish hand stiffened clawlike.

Two feet away from her left foot lay a half-filled bottle of scotch. Blood was smeared on the end of the bottle, and adhering to it were a few strands of gray hair.

I saw one thing more, and a wave of nauseating panic washed over my brain: there was a blood stain on the leg of my trousers and a faint but unmistakable smear on my shoe.

I cursed my carelessness and inefficiency. I had thought I had thoroughly cleaned that up when Helms had gashed my wrist that morning, but I had not known that a damp cloth was not enough and that the stains would reappear.

I turned to Griffin. I knew that my face must have been tinged with green, but I managed to keep a certain control over my voice. "Griffin, I find this very embarrassing."

Griffin said: "I know just how you feel. Let's all sit down, have a drink, and maybe talk a little."

We went back into the living room. The men seated themselves, and I poured some drinks as though we had simply gathered for a friendly poker game.

"Who is she?" I asked.

Of course, I knew who the dead woman was; but if Griffin had not yet identified her, I might be able to avoid talking about the Father Walsh affair at once, giving me the time I thought I needed to think.

"You don't know her?" Griffin asked.

"Never saw her before."

Griffin looked at me as though he were formulating another question; then, with quick change of mind, he nodded to Regan.

Regan put his drink on the desk and went into the bedroom. I heard him take up the telephone. His voice drifted into the room.

He said: "Hello. Come up here. Pronto."

A moment later there was a knock on the door. Regan went quickly to open it. Raymond looked into the apartment.

"Come in," Regan said. "All the way, son."

The clerk bobbed his birdlike head nervously and came to the center of the room. He was very pale; his large Adam's apple and his right cheek twitched to the same tempo. I felt extremely sorry for him.

Griffin said: "We just want you to tell your story again for the benefit of Mr. D'Arcy."

"Yes, sir," the clerk began. "The — the old woman came to the desk and asked if —"

"What time was that?" I asked.

"About ten minutes after four, sir."

Griffin said: "You're just to listen, D'Arcy, not play district attorney." He turned to Raymond. "Go ahead, mister."

"Yes, sir. Well, she asked if Mr. D'Arcy was at home. I said, 'I do not think so, would you care to leave a message?' Then she told me that she is a very good friend of Mr. D'Arcy and —"

"One moment," I interrupted. "I never saw —"

And from Griffin: "I told you to keep quiet!"

The detective glared at me for a moment, then nodded for Raymond to continue his narrative.

"Yes, sir," Raymond continued, "that's right, sir: a very old friend of Mr. D'Arcy, and he is expecting her and would it be possible for me to let her wait upstairs. Well, sir, I looked her over very carefully and I thought I would be all right. What harm could a little old woman who hardly weighs ninety pounds do? And perhaps even Mr. D'Arcy would appreciate the thoughtfulness."

"Did you come in with her?" I asked quickly.

"No, sir. I just opened the door and she went in, and that was the last I saw of her until I came back up here and found her — like that."

Griffin said: "Tell Mr. D'Arcy why you came back up here."

"Yes, sir. It was the switchboard. It started buzzing, I mean. The phone in this apartment. I plugged in and said hello, but no one answered. I disconnected. It started buzzing again, and again I plugged in and said hello, but no one answered.

"By this time, I was a little worried about permitting the little old lady to go up without Mr. D'Arcy's instructions, and I thought I'd better go up to see what was wrong. I knocked on the door, and when she didn't answer I came right in and found her in the bedroom on the floor with the telephone cord in her hand and the phone on the floor beside her. I didn't touch a thing, not a thing, but ran right downstairs and called Police Headquarters."

"You told us she was carrying something under her arm when she came in," said Griffin.

"Yes, sir. She held a book under her arm."

"You thought you knew what kind of a book it was?"

"Yes, sir. A Bible."

Griffin said: "A Bible. Okay. That's all."

Raymond bobbed his head and backed out hastily, with Regan closing the door after him.

Griffin turned to Regan as he returned.

"Frisk him."

Regan slapped my arms up over my head and proceeded to go through my clothes in an extremely efficient manner. From my inner pocket he took the envelope inscribed with the name of Father Walsh and held it out to Griffin.

Regan was down on one knee, running his quick, experienced hands up and down my trouser legs. He halted abruptly and stared at the stains on my cuff and shoe. At that precise moment, I would have given more than a great deal to have been elsewhere.

"D'Arcy's been wading in ketchup," he said in his laconic drawl.

Griffin bent to examine the smears.

"I can explain that."

"Later," said Griffin.

Regan continued to go through my pockets. He discovered the brass tag from the library checkroom, was about to toss it carelessly onto the table, but stopped and examined it with interest. He looked up into my face, started to speak, checked his words, and nodded to Griffin.

Griffin said: "Okay, D'Arcy, let's go."

I decided it might be best to go along quietly. We went out into the hall. Griffin stopped to give some instructions to a uniformed patrolman left standing guard at my door, and then we went into the elevator.

We walked through the lobby, out into the street, and around the corner. There stood the police car. I was seated in the tonneau, Regan and Lucas flanking me on either side. Griffin sat up front with the driver.

"To the Receiving Hospital," said Griffin.

Chapter Four

THE POLICE CAR rolled east one block to Park Avenue, turned south on the avenue as far as Sixty-fourth Street, then east again to Third Avenue, swung south to Fifty-second Street, on which we sped east once more to First Avenue, and then again south along First Avenue until we drew up before that depressing pile of mortar overlooking the East River and known to the average citizen simply as the Receiving Hospital.

Inside, in the hushed and spacious reception room, Lucas and I sat on a cold marble bench while Griffin and Regan bent to talk in whispers to an authoritative-looking nurse seated behind a desk.

I could see Griffin's lips form the words, "thank you," then he nodded across to Lucas, who tapped me gently on the elbow. We rose to our feet and entered the waiting lift, Griffin first and Regan and Lucas drawing up close behind me.

"Ten," said Griffin to the operator.

We left the elevator in the same order as we had entered it and started down the artificially lighted corridor. The air was heavy with ether and astringents and served further to depress me.

A young doctor in civilian dress appeared in the square formed by an intersecting corridor and came forward to meet us. He smiled pleasantly and held out a hand which Griffin took in his own.

"How are you, doc?"

"Fine, Captain. Haven't seen you since the O'Donnell shooting. Shaw goes to the chair next week, doesn't he?"

"Yes. Feel sort of bad about that, too. Nice kid, that Shaw. Took kind of a liking to him. Oh, well . . ."

We came to a halt before a door guarded by a uniformed policeman.

"Well, here we are," said the doctor. "You may go in, Captain, but you must only stay a minute. The poor devil is still alive, but I don't think he can last much longer."

Lying in a white wrought-iron bed, his head and face almost completely swathed in bandages, was a man. An intricate and ominous-looking brace was fastened to the back of his head and neck. His eyes were closed and his breathing labored. I was quite sure I had never seen him before.

The doctor went to the bed and tapped gently on the man's shoulder. He opened his eyes slowly and stared stupidly at the faces of the men in the room.

"What?" he whispered hoarsely.

The doctor bent to his ear and spoke with the penetrating sharpness one uses to reach a rapidly failing consciousness.

"The police want you to look at another man. If this is the man, just say yes. If not, don't bother to say anything. Just close your eyes and go back to sleep."

Regan pushed me close to the bed. The patient looked up into my face for what seemed an eternity. Suddenly, an excitement came into the drug-filled eyes of the man in the bed.

He said: "That's him, that's him!"

The doctor said: "All right. Don't excite yourself. All right, now . . ." He turned to Griffin. "You'd better go now."

The purple clouds in the west had turned an ominous black and the sky had dimmed to the first touches of dusk as the automobile stopped in front of Police Headquarters.

We climbed the steps fronting Centre Street and turned right inside the door and went into a small square room devoid of furniture except for a few chairs.

Griffin locked the door.

Lucas pulled down the shades.

Regan placed a chair in the center of the room directly under a tin lampshade which housed the most enormous light bulb I had ever seen.

"Sit down, D'Arcy," he said.

I sat in the chair. I was very frightened. I fought desperately to prevent myself from falling into complete panic.

"All right, D'Arcy," Griffin said. "Let me hear it."

I thought for a moment. I wanted to tell Griffin everything, but the day's events had been so bizarre, I was convinced that my story would be met with contempt and disbelief. Also it would mean involving the girl. That I did not want to do until I could hear from Barrett. I was determined to keep her clear until after we had had a showdown.

For a moment I was confident, but my confidence received a jolt when I suddenly recalled the man in the hospital. Here was something I did not know: Who was he and why had he identified me?

Griffin suddenly asked:

"How did you get blood on your pants and shoe?"

"From this," I said.

I held aloft my bandaged wrist. Regan started to undo it.

"We'd better look at it," he said. "You may be getting an infection."

He removed the bandage, and the three men bent to examine the laceration. The teeth marks were plainly visible.

Regan said: "Solid bite for an old dame with store teeth."

Lucas put the bandage back and shook his head despairingly.

"When did this happen?" Griffin asked.

"This morning."

"Who did it?"

"I did."

Griffin looked at me in stony silence. "I'm trying God damned hard to be a gentleman," he said grimly. "But I'm beginning to lose my patience. How did you get that?"

"I told you. I did it myself. I was eating corn-on-the-cob and went too far to the right."

Griffin suddenly thrust the brass library check under my nose, and then I remembered where I had seen the man in the hospital. I was deeply shocked, but gave no sign.

"What did you check at the library this morning!"

"Books."

"What books?"

"*Culinary Adventures with Rector* and *Memoirs of Oscar Wilde*."

Griffin's lips tightened, and for an instant he sat in silence as he fought back the desire to strike me.

"You checked a package of books," he said in a laboredly patient tone. "The man you saw in the hospital gave you this tag. A little later he was slugged. His skull was fractured. His neck was broken. He won't live. The gunsel who slugged him took the package you checked. Nothing else. Just those books. What were they, D'Arcy, and who wanted them?"

"I told you the truth. You can check that with my secretary. She delivered them to me at the library."

Griffin hitched his chair closer and put his head forward in an extremely confidential manner. His voice was suddenly soft and friendly, and I recognized this change in tactic as a strategic defeat for Griffin.

He said: "Now, look, D'Arcy — we don't want to make trouble for you. Believe me. But we've got a job to do, and you can help us. Some day you might have something to take care of, and maybe we'll be able to help you. Now let me put it to you straight: Yesterday Father Walsh comes to see you with a yarn about some Bibles and the Walls of Jericho. Last night we find him on the end of a rope. Later, you call me. You say you think the old man was telling the truth and that he might have been murdered. Now we'll take one thing at a time. Why did you think that?"

"Intuition," I said.

"*Ummm!* All right. This morning you check some books at the library. The attendant is slugged, the books taken. This morning you send your girl out to buy a Bible and read to you about the Walls of Jericho.

This morning you talk to Father Walsh's sister on the phone, tell her to come to your apartment. She comes, and with a Bible under her arm. A few minutes later she's a stiff — the Bible gone.

"You come home, blood on your pants, on your shoe. Teeth marks in your wrist. Nineteen hundred dollars in an envelope marked Father Walsh. Refuse to account for your movements during the —"

"*Can't* account —"

"All right. Can't account for your movements during the day. We got two homicides and a third on the way up when that guy in the hospital goes stiff. From where I sit, all that doesn't look so healthy for a guy named D'Arcy. Now, does it?"

Griffin waited for me to speak, but when I maintained my silence, he went on:

"All right. We agree on that. Now I know you don't go in for murder, and I know that you didn't put the bang on anybody. But I also know that you can give me a lot of answers I need. What are these Bibles? What's meant by the Walls of Jericho?"

I opened my eyes and looked at Griffin. "I am not ungrateful to you for the hand of friendship you extend," I said. "But right now I have only one thing to say: Book me or let me go."

Griffin grinned at me. "Bright little lad, eh, D'Arcy? Book you and you'll be out in an hour on a writ." He shook his head and chuckled. "No. You can go home now. Your apartment should be pretty well cleaned up. Unless, of course, you find another stiff waiting for you. Then you can come back here and we'll be glad to put you up for the night."

OUTSIDE THE CITY was dark. A violent midsummer cloudburst had descended, and the streets were swirling, miniature torrents.

I blotted out all effort to think and decided to go to my hotel for the telegram from John Barrett in San Francisco which I was confident would be awaiting me. It was now imperative that I have a showdown with the girl at once.

The windswept rain had increased its fury when

my taxi drew up before the Marlin. I paid the driver and made a run for the lobby.

Inside, seated on the small upholstered bench near the elevator, was Marco. He was wearing a raincoat dating back to the turn of the century, and between his knees he gripped an umbrella. He rose nervously to his feet when he saw me enter and came forward, holding out a limp hand which I ignored.

"I waited a long time for you, D'Arcy. It's about — it's a matter of great importance. About the — the books."

Marco's eyes searched my face anxiously, his tongue playing over his lips. Without speaking, I nodded my head and he followed me into the lift.

The automatic door of the elevator slid open on the seventh floor. We walked down the hall to my apartment. I opened the door. On the floor was a telegram. I invited Marco to have a drink while I read the message. I noted with satisfaction that it fully confirmed my suspicion about the identity of "Rachel."

WESTERN UNION
San Francisco Cal 26

MZ A 906 33/36

D'ARCY
MARLIN APARTMENTS
NYC

RIGHT. SHE IS P. B. AWAY FIVE MONTHS. WHEREABOUTS UNKNOWN. FAMILY MUM. LAST SEEN GREAT DEAL WITH OLAF HEKSTROM LOCAL ART DEALER. HE TOO ABSENT. SHOOT ME THE DIRT SQUIRT.
JOHN

I folded the telegram carefully, placed it in my pocket, and turned to my unexpected guest. He had not taken his eyes from my face all the while I had been reading the message.

"I've had a rather trying day, Marco," I said. "So if you will be brief . . ."

"Yes . . . *Ummmm* . . . I read in the papers about the terrible thing that happened in your apartment.

Terrible, terrible. How could such a thing happen right here in New York? Right in a respectable man's own home? I would never think . . . Terrible, terrible . . ."

He shook his head dolefully.

"What is on that restless mind of yours, Marco?" I asked abruptly.

"Yes . . . on my mind." Marco took a sip of his drink and then looked up into my face. "This afternoon, D'Arcy, you came to my shop and asked me about some Bibles. About the Aelfric Book of Joshua. That is a fact?"

"Go on," I said.

"After you left my shop, I was visited by another man who is also interested in Bibles — yes, especially with an item dealing with Joshua. That is a fact. For a while he hemmed and he hawed, and I listened because I thought he was trying to sell me something. You know what I mean? *Ummmm.* Well, I soon saw he didn't have anything to sell. He wanted to buy. I also learned he had been doing some talking with you. He saw you come into my shop. He told me that. He thought perhaps you were coming to — well, to pick up the — the items. You know what I mean? *Ummmm.* Well, when I saw he didn't have anything to sell, I lost interest in him. Yes. That is a fact. *But —*"

Marco paused impressively and held aloft a stubby forefinger.

"*But,*" he repeated, "I did learn enough from him to convince me that he expects to buy something from *you.* Yes. That is a fact. And — well, that's why I'm here."

Marco leaned back in his chair, sipped his drink nervously, and looked into my face over the rim of his glass.

I said: "I am listening."

Marco put the drink on the small table by his elbow and ran his handkerchief across his head.

"Well, this man offered —"

"Let us call him Helms," I interrupted. "It will make for clarity."

"Good. Helms. Well, he offered me ten thousand

63

for the items. Ten thousand! Can you imagine? I kept a straight face. I'll think it over, I said. Ha! think it over for ten thousand! Now, I know you realize they're worth more. Even so, I'm ready to talk your business your way. How much do you want?"

"Marco," I said, putting forth a cautious feeler, "I am sure you understand how careful I must be at this stage of the game. Particularly after what happened here this afternoon."

Marco bobbed his head in agreement.

"Certainly, certainly."

"And before I can talk further about terms or the — items, you will tell me exactly where you stand in this thing."

Marco looked at me wide-eyed.

"But you know where I stand."

"Of course," I said hastily. "But — but I must know what went wrong. I mean," I added, "with the — the deal."

The little man grinned at me slyly.

"Maybe you know better than I do — eh, D'Arcy? Yes. Since the first contact with London, we never heard a word. It was all arranged — then sudden silence."

"Arranged? You mean the—removal of the items?"

"Yes. And one can't send letters of inquiry about such things. No. You can see that. Naturally, we thought the whole thing had been dropped on the other end as too risky. All over. Forget it. *Caput!* That's what I thought. Until I was visited by the priest — and then you. I don't know what happened — or how you got in. I don't know who this other organization is that's after the items — this Helms. But I made the original contact with London for my client, and it's only right that you should do business with us. Yes. What's honest is honest. That is a fact."

"I see. One thing more, Marco: you will have to tell me who your client is."

"No!"

"I insist."

Marco wrestled with his soul. Then he said:

"All right, D'Arcy. My client is a highly respected citizen. He must never be involved in any — any conversations. That is a fact. You understand?"

"Perfectly."

"All right. You understand. Perfectly. All right. Then I'll tell you." Marco mopped his pate nervously. "Yes. His name is de Brisseaux. Count de Brisseaux."

I made an effort to conceal my shocked surprise.

"Very interesting," I murmured.

Marco rambled on, but I was barely listening.

I felt a hand on my arm and turned to the little man.

"I beg your pardon?"

"And you must remember, D'Arcy," Marco was saying, "that, although I told you what the possible value might be, it depends on a ready market. Yes. That is a fact. And a market for such things is not very easy to find. A *safe* market, I mean. And my offer is very generous, very generous: one hundred thousand for both copies."

For a moment I stood still and pretended to ponder.

"Well, Marco," I said, "the offer is extremely tempting. But just one thing prevents me from accepting."

Marco strained forward anxiously in his chair. A few drops of liquor splashed unnoticed to his trousers.

"Yes?"

"Yes. Just one thing: I haven't got the Bibles."

Before there could be a scene, I went quickly to usher Marco out, swung the door open, and there on the threshold stood Griffin and Regan.

Griffin said: "No, we weren't eavesdropping. I was just about to knock."

I said: "I am sure of that."

The two men brushed past me, walked through the foyer and into the living room. Marco looked from me to the detectives and then back to me apprehensively. I closed the door and joined my guests. I turned to Griffin.

"Won't you come in?"

Griffin said: "Thanks. It's wet outside."

He removed his rain-soaked trench coat and threw it over a chair.

Regan said: "Hello, Marco. How's the swindling going?"

A sickly grin flickered across Marco's lips as he nervously passed his handkerchief over his pate.

I said: "Unfortunately, my friend was just about to leave when you —"

"Yes, yes," Marco put in hurriedly. "I was just about to — well, good night, gentlemen."

Marco started for the door, but Griffin gently took him by the arm and pressed him down into a chair.

Marco had become a jellylike mass of fear, and I could see that even now he half-suspected that in some manner I had tricked him. To save what was left of his own skin, once police pressure was applied, he would most certainly babble at a great rate to Griffin. He would tell him of Helms and of my dealing with him, and this, of course, would quickly lead to Patricia Behrens.

Griffin was forcing my hand. I would have to devise some immediate pretext, or reach a bargain with Griffin which would persuade him to turn Marco loose for the moment.

"Before you go, Griffin, I'd like to talk to you."

The cynical smile on Griffin's face widened. "Why not?"

He followed me into the foyer.

I said: "I was going to call you after Marco left. Let him go for now. I've much to tell you, and after you've listened to me, it will be easier to force Marco to talk. Right now, you don't know what —"

Griffin did not even trouble to hear me out. He shrugged his shoulders carelessly. "Why not?" he said. "I can always find Marco when I want him."

It was that easy; in fact, the very ease with which I had accomplished my purpose should have proved an alert, but my momentary relief dissolved all sense of caution.

We returned to the living room. Marco looked into our faces anxiously. Griffin smiled at him in friendliest fashion and said:

"You can go now, chum."

Marco rose from his chair in slow bewilderment. He ran his tongue across his dry lips and made a futile effort to speak.

"I — I can . . ."

His voice cracked.

Griffin said: "That's right, chum."

Marco slowly turned his gaze upon me, a great distrust in his eyes. Then, mumbling incoherently, he quickly and quietly left the apartment.

I said: "Sit down, gentlemen. This may take a few minutes."

Griffin and Regan made themselves comfortable on the large sofa while I prepared some drinks at the bar.

"Where do you want to begin, D'Arcy?" asked Griffin.

"Well," I said, "last night I deliberately had my paper plant a yarn reading that I had discovered the body of Father Walsh and was on the scene when the police arrived."

"Why did you do that?"

"Intuition." I grinned and this time Griffin grinned back at me. "It bore fruit this morning in the person of one Reverend Sergei Probiloff. He came to my apartment, accompanied by the stand-in for Gargantua, and demanded that I sell him 'the Bibles.'"

Griffin said: "What Bibles?"

"At the moment, I did not know. But I led him to believe that I was fully aware of what he was talking about, and took from him an advance payment, promising to deliver within a few days."

"Where does this Reverend live?"

"I don't know. He is to call me. He said that he had been searching for these Bibles for some time and had finally traced them to Father Walsh.

"When he left," I continued, "I suspected that he would have his ape-man follow me in an effort to find out where I would go to get the books. I called my girl at the office and instructed her to wrap two books and meet me at the library. She did. Probiloff's man saw me take the books and check them. My ruse worked. He no longer followed me. But it worked too well, I'm afraid. He attacked the library attendant and seized the package of books, thinking, of course, that they were the Bibles. That explains the man in the hospital. I'm deeply sorry for that, but . . ."

I lapsed into silence.

"Go on . . ."

"Yes . . . Well, when I reached my office, Catherine Walsh was on the phone. She wanted to see me and we made an appointment to meet here at four o'clock. She arrived too early, and I was too late."

"*Ummmm* . . . Now, if you don't mind, D'Arcy, from here out I'll ask questions. It will be more on the line and much quicker."

"Please do."

"Now — you went from the library to your office and made an appointment with Catherine Walsh. Did you speak to anyone else on the phone?"

"Yes. To Bishop Martin."

"What did you say to Bishop Martin?"

"I made an appointment to see him."

"Then what?"

"Well, I left the office and —"

"No. You sent out for a Bible."

"Oh, yes. I wanted to hear my girl read the passage about the Walls of Jericho. I thought it might give me some clue to the meaning of that cryptic phrase. But I could make nothing of it."

"Then you left the office?"

"Yes. I went to lunch at the Hotel Bolton."

"Is that a usual haunt of yours?"

"I go there occasionally."

"*Ummm*. And then you went to —"

"Oh, I beg your pardon," I interrupted. "I had forgotten; before I went to lunch, I visited Marco in his bookshop."

I then told Griffin of my conversation with Marco in which he had made me aware of the Aelfric Book of Joshua and its history.

"After the two copies had been removed from the British Museum," I went on, "something apparently went wrong with the plot. In some manner which I cannot understand, the Bibles came into the hands of Father Walsh. There are only two copies of the Aelfric Translation, and it is these books which they are seeking."

"They?"

"I mean the Reverend Probiloff and — Marco."

"*Ummm*. I see . . . And the teethmarks on your wrist?"

"That, Captain, is another story."

"Who are you covering, D'Arcy? The gal?"

"What girl?"

Griffin rose to his feet with a sigh.

"Okay, D'Arcy. Half a loaf, I guess, is that much to the good. You told me enough to hit you with sixteen different counts. But I won't. Not now. I think you're just a damned fool. I'm going to check your yarn all along the route. To London and back. And if I find that you're putting the horns on me, I promise you that I — Well, to hell with it."

Griffin went to the door, Regan right behind him. I held the door open for the men to leave.

"I've told you all I could, Griffin."

"Yes. That's what I figured."

The two men left and I closed the door behind them.

I took out the telegram I had received from Barrett and read it again. I would have to hurry. It was very possible that Griffin would discover Helms and Patricia at the Bolton for himself merely by talking with Tiny Stover.

Quickly I changed my damp clothes, downed one short drink, and left the apartment.

I hadn't been in my apartment more than an hour, and the rain still descended in force. As I walked from the lobby into the street, a hand reached out from the dark and pulled me up short.

Standing in the dimmed-out entrance to the hotel, water dripping heedlessly from nose and chin, was Rauch. He gripped my arm firmly, and in this other hand he held forth an envelope. I took it, removed the enclosed note, and held it up to a shaft of light from the lobby:

MR. D'ARCY:

It is most urgent that you come to my hotel. I must speak with you at once. Please do not be difficult. I have instructed your escort to feel free to shoot if you refuse.

SERGEI P

Rauch was now pressing some hard object into my left kidney. Rain streaming from us, we walked to the corner where a taxicab awaited us. We entered, and without a word of instruction, the driver put his machine in motion.

RAUCH KNOCKED on the door of apartment 2240 on the twenty-second floor of the Hotel Carlridge. For a large and cumbersome man, he knocked very gently.

The door was opened by the Reverend Mr. Probiloff, wrapped in a bizarre dressing gown and smelling of attar of roses.

"Come in, Mr. D'Arcy," he said.

I walked into the apartment. Probiloff closed the door behind me, and Rauch unobtrusively disappeared into another room.

The apartment was luxuriously furnished. A Capehart stood in one corner, playing very softly.

"Charming place," I said.

Probiloff's smile widened. "You like it?" His voice was anxious, as though on my opinion rested great decisions. "Do you really like it? It is so difficult to find suitable accommodations in a hotel. Will you join me?"

He gestured to a table in the middle of the room neatly laid with a cold supper.

"Thank you."

I removed my coat, and we seated ourselves at the table. There were generous slices of ham, breast of guinea hen, and an assortment of tangy cheeses. I ate my fill of the excellent food, then settled back comfortably in the soft chair and sipped a whisky. I was extremely tired. Then I said:

"King Kong gave me your note."

"Yes." Probiloff lit a cigar. *"Umm.* Yes. You must forgive my insistence. But I have something here that belongs to you. I thought you might be anxious about them."

He rose to his feet, went to a small table, and took up two books. He held them out to me — *Memoirs of Oscar Wilde* and *Culinary Adventures with Rector.*

I took them and said, "Thank you." I rose to my feet, the books under my arm.

"Why did you check those books, Mr. D'Arcy?"

"I have a peculiar aversion to being trailed by homicidal maniacs."

"I cannot trust you."

"You must not grow bitter," I said lightly.

"Since this morning, things have changed. I do not

intend to stay in New York beyond tomorrow. I can
no longer afford to wait for you. I gave you one
thousand dollars on your promise to deliver. But that
is not important. You may keep that money. Now,
however, it is imperative that you be truthful with me
so that I can guide myself properly. Have you or have
you not got the Bible?"

"Yes," I said in reply to his question. "I have the
Bible."

Probiloff looked at me queerly, a note of puzzlement
in his eyes. Then the muscles in his lean jaws tensed,
and he took a step to me.

"Then you must deliver as you promised."

"In three days. That is our agreement."

"What are you waiting for?"

On sudden impulse, I said: "Helms."

Probiloff displayed no reaction. It was almost as
though this bit of intelligence was no surprise to him.

"You are dealing with Helms," he said flatly.

"Yes."

"What did he promise you?"

"The truth, one of the Bibles, an even split."

"Did you say *one* of the Bibles?"

There was amusement in his voice.

"Yes. I will admit that I succeeded in securing only
one. Helms has the other."

"You are quite sure of that?"

"Quite."

"Did you give him that one?"

"No. That is why I am dealing with him. Tomorrow he will produce it. You may have your money
back."

Probiloff stood quietly, looking into my face. He
appeared greatly perturbed and baffled. Then he went
to the liquor table and poured two drinks. He held one
out to me and smiled.

"Mr. D'Arcy, what do you think those Bibles are?"

"Extremely valuable," I replied.

"But do you know why?"

"Of course."

"No, Mr. D'Arcy — you do *not* know why. Shall I
tell you how I know? Because you said that Helms
offered you, as your share, *one* of the Bibles. That is

impossible. One is valueless without the other." Probiloff paused impressively.

"Please go on," I said.

"Does that not surprise you?"

"I am listening," I said.

Probiloff considered for a moment, as though he were organizing his material in his head.

"You have told me," he resumed, "what Helms has promised you. That I cannot do, because it is not mine to promise. I am going to tell you the truth about everything: the Bibles, Helms, myself.

"I am not a bibliophile. I am a missionary. No doubt you will think it strange that I have used such, ah, such untoward tactics. But I am on my greatest mission, one to which I have dedicated my life, if need be — and I am contending with ruthless people. Helms and I have been in conflict for many years in the search for these Bibles.

"At one time," he continued, "he thought I had them; and poor Rauch was seized, his tongue torn from his mouth at Helms's instigation because he would not tell where they were. He could not tell. I did not have them.

"These Bibles, Mr. D'Arcy, belong to a wealthy set of Coptic Christians in the interior of India. These natives were converted many years ago by a missionary named Reverend Emilio Balcito, an Italian who devoted the greater part of his life to an effort to convert these people because they wield great influence over a vast number of natives throughout the interior.

"A wave of prosperity followed their conversion, and, although it was pure chance, of course, the natives associated this with Father Balcito. They grew to love him, and on his deathbed he gave to their priests two Bibles which were his during his life. The Bibles were placed on an altar where the people came to worship. They had become sacred to them. But one day they were gone — stolen. The people were thrown into a panic, and were convinced that great misfortune would follow.

"The priests have offered fabulous sums for their recovery. I know those people well, Mr. D'Arcy. I have worked among them, and I have taken upon myself the mission of finding the Bibles. Not for the money, not for any material rewards, but to help those natives, so newly won, to help them retain their faith in Christianity." Probiloff stopped speaking and sipped his drink.

"And what about Mr. Helms?"

"Helms was a businessman, trading in India. He heard about the Bibles and, being an adventurer at heart, decided to search them out. He intends to bleed the priests of everything they have. And he knows that they will pay. Yes ... And those are the Bibles marked *E. B.* — the initials of Reverend Emilio Balcito." Probiloff rose to his feet and placed his glass on the liquor table.

"And what about the Walls of Jericho?"

Probiloff looked at me blankly. "I beg your pardon?"

I rose to my feet wearily and placed the glass on a table. I started to go, but Probiloff placed himself squarely in my path.

"What do *you* know about the Walls of Jericho?" he asked.

"Only that a chap named Joshua *blitzed* them and the walls came tumbling down."

I put my hand on his chest, pushed gently and swept him aside. Then I saw Rauch standing at the door. In his right hand he held his revolver. It was pointed at my head. I turned to look at Probiloff, and a great rage welled up within me.

I said: "This is growing tiresome." I seized the surprised Probiloff by the arm and, in the same move, spun him across the room. He crashed into the mute, throwing the man with the gun off balance.

I lunged forward almost before Probiloff had struck Rauch, seized the gun hand, and bent it back. I heard the wrist bone snap, and Rauch screamed horribly with the pain. The gun thudded to the carpet.

Probiloff dived for it, but I fetched him a solid kick under his left jaw with the heel of my shoe. He lay still. I scooped up the gun. With one arm dangling, the giant mute made a wild rush for me. I stepped aside and smashed him full in the face with the butt of the gun as he thundered by. He dropped like a poled ox, right cheek open to the bone, blood seeping into the carpet.

I bent to examine the pair, and it was evident that I need not worry about them for the next few minutes. Quickly I went from room to room, searching the apartment from floor to ceiling and from wall to wall. In a sleeping chamber, on a closet shelf, I found a black brief case. It contained a number of photographs of various canvases done by Renoir, Gauguin, Picasso. There were also seven letters addressed to the Reverend Sergei Probiloff at the General Post Office Delivery in various cities of the United States. Only one of these letters held any interest for me. It was a typed note of recent date, brief and unsigned:

Definite E. B. died N. Y. Hid real identity during last years. Find no death certificate under name. Undoubtedly buried under assumed identity. Have discovered he was attended at death by priest named Father Walsh. Positive B. gave him Bibles. Am working closely with little man and he is hot. Advise you to come at once.

That was all.

I folded the note carefully and placed it in my pocket. A definite pattern was beginning to form in my mind.

I tried the knob of the second closet in the room but the door was locked. Suddenly a dull thumping sounded from the interior of the closet. I listened carefully, and the thumping continued.

I returned to my unconscious host, removed from his pocket a key ring. One of the keys fitted the lock on the door of the closet. I threw the door open. There, on the floor, lay Patricia. She was bound hand and foot and a gag was pressed into her mouth. She had been hammering at the door with the heel of her shoe.

I bent quickly and removed the gag. She inhaled deeply and a bit of color returned to her face.

"Well, don't just stand there looking like Civic Virtue," she said, and there was a note of hysteria in her voice. "Get me out of here!"

As I unbound her hands and feet, I asked her what had happened, but she refused to answer my questions until she had had a cup of coffee and a cigarette.

"How did you know I was here?" she asked.

She shook the cords from her ankles, and I helped her to her feet.

"I didn't," I replied.

"Then —?"

Rauch's huge figure appeared in the doorway. One hand hung limp, but in the other was a gun. He was still suffering the numbing effects of the blow I had dealt him, and his hand was unsteady as he raised the weapon.

Probiloff, in the next room, could not rise quickly enough to prevent him from pulling the trigger. I heard the explosion and a bullet went by my head and out through the window. I threw myself forward against the door and slammed it shut in Rauch's face.

Quickly the girl came to my help, and we managed to barricade the door with a heavy chest which stood near by. In a moment the weight of the two men was thrown up against the door, but our defense held.

Patricia looked about the room and then went quickly to the wide window. She threw it open.

"There's a fire escape!"

"Splendid! And the wettest storm you ever saw," I added.

I seized the girl by the arm, pushed her out onto the fire escape, and followed close behind. I lowered the window after us. The rain pelted down.

We had descended about three floors and were standing before a closed window of an apartment. I peeked through the pane, and a small light inside disclosed a bedroom. There was no one present.

The window slid open easily. I crawled into the room and helped the girl in after me.

We crossed the bedroom soundlessly, leaving a trail of water after us. I opened the door leading to the hall and we succeeded in catching a descending elevator which took us to the lobby. We went out into the street and hurried into a taxi. I gave the driver the Hotel Bolton as his destination and leaned back on the cushions to recover my breath.

Chapter Five

ATRICIA CAME OUT of her bedroom. She was snugly wrapped in a terryrobe and about her head was wound a large towel. She rubbed this briskly into her hair as she collapsed in a chair close to me.

"Well!" she said, blowing hard. "That's a little better!"

I was seated on the sofa, looking like a road-company Buddha, no doubt, with my legs crossed under me and wrapped in a heavy blanket. My clothes were hung up to dry. At my elbow was a warm drink, and I had to admit that I was beginning to feel better.

I had called Police Headquarters. Griffin had not been there, but I had advised the authorities of Probiloff's address and told them that he would be wanted for murder. I did not think, however, that they would find the Reverend at home when they called.

In the center of the room stood a large trunk. Much of its contents were on the floor in a scattered state. A few bags lay about, and these, too, gave the appearance of having been hurriedly ransacked.

Patricia fixed a highball for herself and then turned to me.

"Now suppose you tell me what you were doing at that apartment."

"Never mind what I was doing there," I said crossly. "Right now I want to know how you succeeded in trussing yourself up and crawling into the Reverend Probiloff's closet."

"I can't take all the credit for that. I had help. Yes, from the Reverend and his watchdog."

"I am listening."

"There isn't much to tell. I returned to my apartment this afternoon. I found them here, and you can see what they did." She gestured to the luggage. "They held a gun to me and demanded that I give them the Bible."

"They asked only for one?"

"Yes. I told them I did not have it, and they forced me to go along with them."

"*Ummmm*. Go on . . ."

"Well, I was petrified and they took me to the apartment. There, Probiloff told me that he *knew* I had one of the Bibles, and that if I didn't turn it over to him at once — Well, the usual threats and all that. I finally convinced Probiloff that I do *not* have a Bible, and then he turned to Rauch and said he had better bring you to the apartment for a talk. Then I was trussed up and put in the closet. And that is all I know."

I glanced at the luggage in the room. "You've certainly picked yourself a very wet night for travel. Where were you going?"

"I— Away."

"Where?"

"I don't know."

She lifted her head and her eyes met mine. There was more than a hint of panic in them. "I'm afraid."

"Of what?"

"I think I've been left alone."

"What do you mean?"

"I can't find — Mr. Helms. He — I think he went away. I'm afraid I'm going to be murdered next."

I said: "I should say that your chances are excellent."

She burst into tears, sobbing loudly and with no attempt at restraint. "What shall I do?" she cried.

"Try telling me the truth.'

She sat with her hands in her lap, the palms turned upward, and the tears streaming unheeded down her lifted face.

"Very well. You shall have the truth. Everything. How much do you already know?"

"Start from the beginning. I'll tell you when to stop."

She stared into her glass, then looked up.

"For many years," she began, "my father dealt in rare —"

"That's enough!" My patience was at an end. "Ernst Helms is not your father, and his name is not Ernst Helms. He is Olaf Hekstrom, an art dealer from San Francisco. You're Patricia Behrens, the daughter of Henry Behrens." I went to my clothes, took from a pocket the telegram I had received from Barrett, and tossed it into her lap. She stared down at it without touching it. "You suddenly became very chummy with Hekstrom — or Helms — and then you and he disappeared. No one in 'Frisco knows where you are or what you are doing. That wire is from John Barrett. You know him: the society editor of the *Ledger*. I've gone through too much to cover you with the police in this town. But now I am finished! You'll either tell me the complete truth, or I will wire Barrett a story of your involvement in wholesale murder that will turn Snob Hill over on its peak!"

Patricia looked up at me. Her eyes were now clear and determined and looked into mine frankly.

"All right," she said swiftly, without thinking, "it doesn't matter any more. I don't know any more what is happening or what to do, and I'm sorry I started the whole thing. Yes, it *is* all my fault. His letter said there would be blood, that there would be murder. He was right . . . he was right . . ."

Her voice melted away and she sat very still, staring down at the floor.

"Whose letter?" I asked.

"Elias Behrens."

"Behrens?"

" The artist."

"But your name is also — was he. . . .?"

"He was my grandfather. And that's how it all began."

"Look here," I said impatiently, "if your about to embark upon another of your —"

"No," she interrupted, taking a step to me. "I am telling you the truth. Please listen to me. Yes, Elias

Behrens was my grandfather. Today his name is spoken with those of Renoir, Van Gogh, Degas. You know all that, of course."

"Of course."

"Yes. Who doesn't?" Her voice had grown bitter. "Today the whole art world knows Behrens. But they know little, and are concerned less, with the way he was forced to live before his work was acclaimed; how he struggled and starved, asking only to be permitted to paint in peace."

"Please go on," I said.

"Yes . . . Well, eventually came the day when Elias Behrens, the young, sensitive artist, could no longer bear the coldness with which he and his work were treated — and he disappeared. One day he just walked away from his wife and son and simply disappeared. No one knew where. No one cared very much, really, except his wife and child, and to this day no one knows what happened to him. He was never heard of again, and no more of his work seen."

Her narrative came to a halt again, and she paced the floor nervously. In a low voice she continued:

"I never saw my grandfather. But my father, his son, told me a great deal about him, and I was hurt and shocked, perhaps naïvely, and deeply revolted at the thought that the world could so ill-use a man of such great genius."

"It was not the first time," I murmured.

"I know; but this time it struck very close to home. You see, the few Behrens canvases extant are so very rare that not even my father, with all the wealth he managed to collect, can buy one for himself. Those who own them simply will not sell. And I made up my mind that I would some day write a biography of Elias Behrens to show these smug people, and the world, what they had done to a fine artist, the kind of life he had been forced to lead." She stopped for a moment, smiled briefly: "You see, I am not quite as feather-brained as I had pretended to be. But never mind."

She sipped her drink and paused while she collected her thoughts. I said nothing.

"Finally, I got all the information I could from my father, then I started out to visit all the places where Elias Behrens had lived and worked. I managed to unearth old friends, art dealers who had known him. They were very old and remembered little things about him. I found old letters, scraps of old journals. And then I made a startling discovery. Yes. I discovered that in his dying days, Elias Behrens had painted a mural."

"A mural? But Behrens never did paint a mural!"

"That is what the world believes. But in his last days — embittered, starving, frustrated — he painted a mural on the wall of the hovel in which he lived. Can't you see? That mural would be priceless!"

I succeeded in maintaining a calm, unruffled exterior. "And what does that have to do with the murder of Father Walsh and his sister?"

Patricia said: "Please — let me finish. From the letter I found, it was obvious that my grandfather had turned to the Bible for consolation. I — I think that — it's possible that his mind had been affected toward the end by all that he had suffered during his life. And for his last work he chose as his subject Joshua and his armies about to attack Jericho. He called it, of course, *'The Walls of Jericho.'*

"He knew that he was dying, and he spent the last pennies he could scrape together for paints, denying himself food so that he might finish this mural. When it was completed, he covered the work with a coat of paint, knowing it could be restored — no matter how often it might be painted over."

"And — *that* is the 'Walls of Jericho'?" I asked.

"Yes."

"But — the Bibles! The Aelfric Book of Joshua!"

"I don't know what you are talking about — and I didn't know when you mentioned that name this afternoon."

"You mean that this has nothing to do with — that the Aelfric Book . . . and there was no theft of —" I broke off. "Oh, my God!" Menacing visions of Griffin's face floated before my eyes.

"What is it?" Patricia asked.

"Nothing — only that I told the police that . . ." Again my voice expired.

"When Behrens disappeared," she continued, "no

one knew where he went, where he lived, or where he died. And no one now knows where he painted that mural. He had planned it that way. The only way in which a clue to the location of the mural could be found was to first find his two Bibles. I didn't even know where the Bibles were. And that is when I went to Hekstrom and told him the entire story. He was convinced that this was so, grew very excited, and gave up everything else to help me search for the Bibles and the mural. And he warned me that we must keep our knowledge secret."

"Especially from the Reverend Probiloff."

"He is not a Reverend. Hekstrom told me that Probiloff is a notorious dealer in stolen canvases and forgeries. But in some way, although we were extremely careful, he learned what we were after. He assumed the identity of a Reverend, thinking it might help him in his search for the Bibles. Well, after a long and costly hunt, we finally learned that my grandfather had died somewhere in New York City."

I got to my feet. "All right. And Father Walsh attended him at his death, and Behrens gave the Bibles to the Priest. Is that it?"

"Yes. I spoke with Father Walsh on the telephone the day he — he died."

I asked suddenly: "Did Helms — or Hekstrom — visit the priest before you talked with him on the telephone?"

"No. I don't think so. At first Father Walsh did not seem to know what I was talking about. I could not mention any name because we were sure he had lived and died under an assumed identity. But when I insistently spoke of the Bibles, he seemed suddenly to remember. He said that many, many years ago — Well, he thought he did remember a man who had given him *two* Bibles."

"Did he tell you the man's name?"

"No. I was so excited, I didn't ask then — and made an appointment to come to the priest's home. Well, I did — and you know what happened."

"Is there any way you can prove that what you have told me is the truth?" I asked.

Patricia went to a bag, lifted it to the table, opened

it, and took out a paper which she held out to me.

"This was all I could find of it."

The paper was brittle and yellowed with age. It was part of a scrawled letter torn across the top half:

... live only to finish my greatest work, my only mural. And there will come the day when men will again spill blood for the Walls of Jericho as did Joshua and his hosts. But only in my Bibles will be found the key, and he who reads each word of God will uncover the sweeping vision on the wall of my hovel; glory to God and cursed be all men!

I looked up slowly. I was convinced of two things: that this was *it*, and that I would have to do something before Griffin and his wrath descended upon me.

I folded the letter carefully and placed it in my pocket. "I am going to keep this."

She offered no objection.

I took up the telephone and gave the operator the number of Bishop Martin's residence. I glanced at my watch as I heard the insistent ring on the other end: it was well after midnight.

A woman's sleepy and querulous voice said: "Hello?"

"This is Mr. D'Arcy. I must talk to the Bishop."

The Bishop's voice cut in from an extension: "All right, Mary. I will speak. Mr. D'Arcy?"

I waited until I heard the housekeeper put her telephone away, and then said:

"Yes, Bishop Martin. I know it is late. I know that you are probably in bed. But I am not apologizing for calling, nor am I going to ask permission to see you. I am simply telling you that I am on my way over."

Bishop Martin said: "One moment, Mr. —"

"You must be ready to leave the house when I arrive," I continued sharply. "We have some place to go. You're no doubt aware of what happened to Catherine Walsh in my apartment this afternoon. You must *know* that Father Walsh was murdered. If you had listened to me when I called on you this afternoon, we might at least have prevented the murder of his sister. Now I must insist that you do as I say. I'll be at your residence in half an hour. Please be ready to leave."

There was a troubled silence at the other end. My abrupt attack had shaken the Bishop. "Very well, Mr.

D'Arcy. I will expect you," he said finally.

I thanked him, put the telephone down, and turned to Patricia.

"I'll be with you in a minute," she said crisply.

She started quickly for the bedroom, but I took her arm as she went past me and swung her about. She was very close to me now, her head tilted back, her lips parted. I took her into my arms and started to kiss her gently.

I said: "How soon did I say I would meet the Bishop?"

Patricia said: "In six months."

I said: "How inconvenient."

We kissed again.

Ten minutes later Patricia went into the bedroom to dress while I slipped into my damp and rumpled clothes.

"I don't suppose you were able to find any record of the death or burial in New York of Elias Behrens?" I called out.

"No. None at all," Patricia answered from the other room.

Shortly afterward we left the apartment.

THE BISHOP LIFTED his eyes from his desk and drew his dressing gown a bit tighter about his neck. His face was sleep-puffed and mottled, the muscles limp and tired. Patricia leaned forward anxiously, as though about to speak, but I placed a restraining hand on her arm and she settled back.

"No, Mr. D'Arcy," said Bishop Martin finally, "I am sorry, but I cannot feel it is right to do as you ask."

Again Bishop Martin's eyes fell at once to the desk, and this note of vacillation I found encouraging.

"You must do as I ask," I insisted quietly.

He came sharply to his feet as he spoke. "But — this story of Behrens and the mural is utterly fantastic!"

"I quite agree; utterly and insanely fantastic."

"But it is the truth!" said Patricia.

"And again I agree," said I. "The utter and insane

truth. Please read this." I gave the Bishop the Behrens letter which Patricia had unearthed, and as he read, I continued: "I am convinced that it *is* the truth: the kind of truth which is forced to plead for belief — just as Father Walsh had pleaded — but is refused belief because of its quality of the bizarre and fantastic."

Bishop Martin finished reading the letter, and I could see that his interest had been aroused. He held out the paper and I took it and put it back into my pocket.

"Perhaps you are right," said he. "Perhaps I do not have the imagination. That, however, is not the issue; it is not for us to determine whether or not this is the truth. That is a matter for the police." I made an attempt to speak, but the Bishop hurried on: "I'm sorry. Yes. But I find it impossible to agree to your suggestion that we take it upon ourselves to search the residence of Father Walsh. Our only course is to notify the police of this development at once."

"That is exactly what we must *not* do!" I said with some exasperation. "Not yet. Can't you see? This is the one time when the proper procedure would be most improper. Once the police — and that means the press! — are made aware of this, it will give the killer sufficient warning to flee, if he has not already done so. Either that, or he will make no further effort to secure the second Bible."

"But how can we be sure that he does not already have *both* Bibles?" the Bishop objected.

"I *know* that one Bible is still missing because efforts are being made to find it. If I can discover the second Bible, I know that I can use it to smoke out the killer, whoever he is."

Bishop Martin looked into my face, and the vacillation was no longer in his eyes. He had reached his decision.

"Very well. We will go. But only on one condition: we notify the police whether we do or do not find this second Bible."

I saw that this was the best I could hope to do with Bishop Martin, and to his condition I was forced to agree.

Bishop Martin nodded his acceptance of the pact, and excused himself for a few minutes to change into his street clothes. He returned fully dressed. He was accompanied by the oldish young man with the high celluloid collar and the patent-leather shoes.

"My car is in front of the house," said the Bishop. "Mr. Ricard Biamonte, my secretary, will drive."

I nodded to Mr. Ricard Biamonte, and Mr. Ricard Biamonte acknowledged the salutation by a simple flicker of his long lashes over his dark eyes.

A half-hour later we were gliding through Greenwich Village, into Hudson Street. The youth at the wheel expertly maneuvered the heavy car through the blinding rain into the narrow and mud-gutted driveway of the church grounds.

The car came to a halt directly before the steps leading into the late Father Walsh's residence. Except for a faint blue light which could be dimly seen through the lower bay window, the house was completely dark.

"Please wait here for me, Ricard," said the Bishop.

"Yes, sir," replied Ricard.

We left the car and started up the stairs. I made it a point to avoid placing my weight on the step which creaked. I did not want to hear that sound just then.

Bishop Martin raised the ancient brass knocker and let it fall with a resounding clang. He was obliged to repeat the summons before we heard a shuffling step on the other side of the door, and a voice asked:

"Who is it, now?"

"Please open the door, Miss Brigid," said Bishop Martin.

The housekeeper shot back the bolt and opened the door only enough to permit her to peer out cautiously.

"Oh, your Rivirince!" she said, unlatching the guard chain and throwing the door wide.

"You may go back to your bed, Miss Brigid," said the Bishop.

We entered the gloomy hall, now lit only by the flickering candle carried by the housekeeper. The housekeeper started for the stairs leading to her quarters.

Patricia and I followed the Bishop into the study. He went directly to the wall switch and threw the overhead lights into life. During the next hour, we made a thorough and exhaustive search of the study, library, and sleeping chamber once occupied by Father Walsh. We found nothing remotely resembling the Bible which we were seeking. Feeling more than a little discouraged, I suggested that we try the upper floors, but Bishop Martin stood in the center of the study, a new comprehension growing in his eyes.

"You have thought of something," I said.

At the moment, I did not know why, but the look in the Bishop's eyes served to further deepen my sudden depression.

"Yes ... of course," he whispered to himself. "How stupid of me ... How incredibly stupid of me!"

"What is it, sir?" I asked anxiously.

Bishop Martin turned to me.

"You say that *two* Bibles were given to Father Walsh by a dying man?"

"That is the story."

My fears increased, and it was only through great exertion of will that I forced myself to Bishop Martin's next words:

"And Catherine Walsh was bringing one of these Bibles to you when she was murdered?"

"Yes."

Bishop Martin nodded his head gravely, settled on his heels and folded his hands behind his back.

"Then we need not search any further. Here or any other place."

I leaned forward anxiously.

"Why not?"

"Because that other Bible is nowhere on this earth."

I looked at the Bishop in some bewilderment.

"But — we know that the Father had it. What could he have done with it?"

"What any other priest would have done, my son," replied the Bishop. "He was given two Bibles by a man he attended in his last moments. One Bible he kept. But the other, he blessed and *buried* with that man!"

I cannot now recall with any degree of clarity my

immediate reactions. I know only that a sudden loud buzzing set up inside my head, and that I reached like an automaton for the arm of a chair into which I sank slowly.

"Your only hope," said the Bishop "is to discover the grave of this man Elias Behrens."

"Yes. That is the only hope." I sighed deeply and turned to Bishop Martin: "No, I am afraid it is quite impossible. We haven't the faintest idea under what name he lived and died or under what name he was buried or where he was buried. There's nothing for it. I shall simply have to call Captain Griffin and accept the consequences of bungling the entire case, withholding vital information, and perhaps giving the killer an opportunity to make good his escape. I might even be held accountable in some manner for the death of Catherine Walsh."

I went with heavy tread to the telephone and dialed the number of Police Headquarters. Patricia and the Bishop stood by, watching me silently.

"Police Headquarters? I want to speak to — to Captain Griffin."

I was told that Griffin was not in but was expected back later. I said I would call him again and then put the telephone away.

"Bishop Martin," I said, "Captain Griffin will not be in until later tonight. But I feel that I cannot go through any more this evening. If you agree, I will call for you at your residence at nine tomorrow morning, and we will then go to Headquarters where I will confess everything."

Bishop Martin looked at me compassionately. "Of course, my son," he said. "You meant well and I understand. It is just unfortunate that — well, no matter now. I shall expect you tomorrow morning."

"Thank you, Bishop Martin."

We left the house and returned to the Bishop's car. I refused his kind offer to drive me home, telling him that I would take a cab from the nearest hack stand.

We found an empty taxi a few blocks from the church and, again assuring him that I would be prompt the next morning, I said good night, and Patricia and I got into the cab.

"To the *Morning Post*," I said to the driver.

"What are you going to do?" asked Patricia as we drove off.

"I can no longer bear the strain of this thing," I replied. "And I have no intention of paying another visit to Police Headquarters unless I am absolutely forced to do so. We are going to my office. I shall then call the police and leave word for Griffin that I am waiting for him there. I will find it much easier to say what I must say in my own bailiwick. It will at least give me some confidence and the momentary illusion of security."

Patricia inclined toward me impulsively.

"Oh, you poor darling," she breathed. She kissed me softly on the cheek. "I feel so miserable for you. Oh, I do, I do!"

Susan looked up from behind her typewriter. Her face was haggard and worn, a carbon smear across her forehead. She was elbow-deep in manuscript — on her desk, on the floor, and a great deal more piled neatly on the shelves around the room.

Patricia looked at me inquiringly as we entered the office. "The night-shift?" she asked.

"With the Duchess, all things are possible."

"But what is she doing here at three A. M.?"

"I fear to ask."

Susan came quickly to the front of the desk, a sheaf of papers in one hand, a Bible in the other.

"Oh, Mr. D'Arcy, I'm so glad you came. I'm just beginning to run out of paper and carbon, and I'm only halfway through *Luke!*"

I closed my eyes.

"What," I asked fearfully, "what mad, fever-induced mischief is this?"

"Why, I'm just working, sir."

I opened my eyes slowly.

"You are just working." I looked about at the reams of manuscript. "But what, my cherished one that walks and talks like other normal beings, precisely what are you doing with the Bible?"

"Making a synopsis."

"Come here, my child," I said. "Are you telling me that you have been here at this desk since I left you early yesterday afternoon?"

"Yes, sir!"

"And in all that time you have been engaged in preparing a synopsis of the Bible?"

"Yes, sir! I'm doing it because you asked me to."

"Because I —?"

"Yes, sir. When you went out yesterday afternoon I asked you what I should do with the Bible I bought, and you told me to make a synopsis and leave it on your desk."

I settled back slowly on my heels. I could feel the last pools of resistance draining from my body and I was left with a peculiar sensation of numbness.

"Susan," I said, and my voice seemed very remote, "you may go home now. Yes, please go home now, get into bed, and stay there until I call you."

Susan looked up at me uncertainly and left immediately.

I turned to Patricia. "Please do not ask for an explanation. There is none for Susan. Just accept what has happened without question while I call Griffin."

I could hear the signal being received on the police switchboard, and I waited for a response. Patricia, her head bent over the papers, chuckled.

"Oh, my dear," she laughed, "can't you just see it? This is priceless!" She read Susan's manuscript:

"Once there was a man in the Bible named Joshua. His father's name was Nun. Now this here Joshua Nun wanted to be a great general, and so he got a large army to attack a city in the Bible named Jericho. He sent some —"

I dropped the telephone, came quickly to the girl, and snatched the papers from her fingers. I read the lines with growing excitement and then looked up at the bewildered Patricia.

"Patricia, my lovely, I have always had a profound respect for my womanly intuition. Pray, my pet, with every 'so be it' and 'amen' at your command that this time it is not playing me false!"

I took the startled girl by the hand and swept out of the office.

AT NO TIME, of course, can one consider New York City's Municipal Building in lower Manhattan a place in which one might expect to find an appreciable amount of cheer or warmth. But at four o'clock on a desolate and rainswept morning, it is a bleak morgue housing countless dead statistics.

Patricia and I stood in the wide entrance. We hugged the bronze doors in an effort to escape the lash of the rain which had now attained gale pitch. I pushed the small button marked "night bell" and could hear the brazen clang of the gong within. The door was opened by Murph, the night watchman.

Inside, the corridors were dimly lighted, and it was not until I spoke that Murph recognized me. I had dealth with him on other occasions when it had been necessary to gain access to certain records.

"Murph," I said, "I've come for your help."

"What in the unholy name of all the divils of Bashan brings you here in this storm and at this hour!"

"Trouble, Murph. I want you to let me take a look at the death records."

Murph brought his hand up to his head and slowly rubbed the lobe of his ear between thumb and forefinger. He started to mutter his routine objections, but when I pressed a tip into the palm of his other hand, he turned without a word and led us down the hall to a door which bore the legend "Bureau of Vital Statistics."

Murph inserted his pass-key into the lock, opened the door, and, by the beam of his hand torch, led us into the block-square, high-ceilinged section called the Bureau of Records. Hundreds of massive steel filing cabinets ranged squarely and endlessly in every direction from the center of the cement floor to all the four walls.

Murph said: "I don't want to turn on any lights. You'll have to work with my flashlight."

"That will be sufficient. Take us to the Ns."

"What year?"

"I'm not sure, Murph. About fifty years ago."

"*Ummmmm*. That would be . . ."

"1890 . . . '92 . . ."

Murph thought for a moment, then led us silently through the narrow alleys formed by the shoulder-high cabinets. Patricia's heels made sharp little clicks on the cement floor, and in the absolute quiet it sounded like the popping of penny firecrackers.

Murph halted and played his torch over the section for which I had asked. "This what you want?"

I took the light from Murph's hand and examined the white cards on the face of the cabinets. I focused the beam on the exact card for which I had been searching.

"Yes . . . yes," I whispered. "This is what I want." I gave the torch to Patricia: "Hold the light over the file while I go through it."

It did not take long. I had examined only four or five entries when I stopped and took the torch from Patricia's hand. I withdrew from the case the rectangular card and held it close to the beam of light. I looked up at Patricia. Her face was strained. She had dug her fingers deep into my arm.

"Well?" she breathed.

I nodded and held forth the card. Patricia seized it eagerly. I played the light over it for her to read:

A-24X244L

STATE OF NEW YORK

Department of Health of The City of New York

BUREAU OF RECORDS

Place of Death......Bellevue Hospital.................
Character of Premises......City Hospital.............
Full Name of Deceased......Joshua Nunn.............
Sex ......M...................Color ......W...........
Single, Married, Widowed or Divorced........Unknown
Less than 1 day
Date of Birth......Unknown........................
Age ..70(?) Yrs......Mos......Ds......Hrs......Min.
Occupation ......Unknown ....

SPECIAL INFORMATION

(required in deaths in hospitals and institutions)
Usual Residence ......Unknown.....................
Date of Death......Dec. 24, 1892....................
Cause of Death......Pneumonia.....................
Final Disposition......Buried St. Francis's Cemetery by
Catholic Charities—Father Walsh Attending...........
Certified by......Coles Trapnell M.D.......

N.B.—Case found unconscious by Patrolman Lewis Morton, #7460, in lavatory of Museum of Art on 12/22/92.
C.T.

Patricia looked up from the death certificate. Her face was white, and in her eyes was shock. "D'Arcy — do you think . . . ?"

"There's no doubt about it." I took the card from her fingers and returned it to its proper place in the file. "We were sure he died in this city. There had to be some record. But what name? That letter of his you found showed that in his last days he had been obsessed by the subject of Joshua — the son of Nun. And it took Susan to make it read Joshua Nun. He was found in the Museum of Art — and what more fitting place for Elias Behrens to haunt? And when he was asked his name before he died, in his delirium all he could think of was *Joshua Nun;* the rest, unknown . . . Yes, Patricia, it's all there — even to Father Walsh's name."

I turned to Murph to give Patricia an opportunity to recover her poise.

"Murph, do you happen to have any of your guests available now?"

Murph looked at me blankly.

"Guests?"

"Now don't play coy with me, Murph." It is a well-known fact among the less affluent denizens of the Bowery that for a very modest fee, Murph will permit them a night's lodging in the basement of the Municipal Building. "If you can find two guys who would be willing to turn their hands to a little nocturnal digging in this rain, they can earn fifty dollars — and as much for you if you can supply me with the men and three stout shovels and picks. Can you help me?"

"All right," Murph said, "I'll do what I can."

"Fine! . . . And by the way, Murph, do you know where St. Francis's Cemetery is located?"

"Why, yes. It's that little buryin' ground right back of St. Francis's Church down on Grove Street."

I came to an abrupt halt and gazed stupidly into Murph's face.

"But that's Father Walsh's church!" exclaimed Patricia.

I smiled feebly.

"Yes, my dear. So it is . . ."

The two vagrants recruited by Murph stood shoulder-deep in the rectangular hole which they had dug into the muddy earth behind St. Francis's Church. The ground was soft and thoroughly rainsoaked, and it had not been difficult for us to excavate the grave identified by a weatherbeaten cross as housing the remains of one Joshua Nunn.

Patricia and I stood at the edge of the pit while the men worked. The electric torch which I held gave off only a dim light, barely penetrating the heavy rain which descended like water spilling over a dam.

One of the diggers looked up into the beam of light and there was an excitement in his voice: "Hey, boss — I think we hit it!"

Neither Patricia nor I spoke while the laborers applied hammer and chisel to the cover of the casket. The wood was badly time-rotted and worm-eaten, and great chunks would tear loose from the lid wherever pressure was applied.

Just as the interior of the coffin was to be exposed to view, Patricia turned her head away, and there, inside, we saw the clean white skeleton of a man. Under the long finger bones and resting on the hollow ribs lay a book.

My eagerness overcame any revulsion I ordinarily might have felt, and I reached down and asked one of the diggers to hand it to me. It was a Bible — a mildewed, worm-nibbled Bible; and on its slimy cover were stamped the initials *E. B.*

A wave of elation swept me as I held the Book aloft. I turned to Patricia, but before I could speak the beams of a powerful searchlight swept the area and lit up the scene like daylight. My reflexes were not very alert and, with the others, I swung about and gaped stupidly into the sudden illumination.

Patricia seized my arm, I remember, and my two helpers turned and fled into the darkness. A hoarse voice shouted something that sounded like: "Stop or I'll shoot!" Then three shots were fired — all, I later learned, missing their mark.

The next thing I remember is that Patricia and I

were surrounded by police — or so it seemed at the time, although there were only two. They had been attracted by our light while passing the grounds in their prowl car.

They took in the scene: the violated grave and the open casket; and never have I seen such contempt in the eyes of men.

"Body snatchers, eh!"

"See here, officer," I began.

"Sheddep! Yuh kin tell it down at Headquarters!"

I gripped the Bible tightly under my coat and recited three Hail Mary's and two Our Father's.

Patricia and I sat in Griffin's office, our eyes fastened anxiously on his face. I was surprised and moved by the change which had come over it since we had talked only a few hours ago: it was pinched and haggard, and in his eyes lay a great weariness. He seemed to have lost much of his nervous strength, and, as he sat with his elbow on his desk, his eyes now covered by his hand, an air of resignation cloaked his bent shoulders like a shawl.

The arresting policemen had just made known to the detective my latest act of lawlessness, and Griffin had dismissed them, saying he wanted to be alone with Patricia and me. I had not yet made my explanations to him, and for a long moment after the policemen had left the office, Griffin merely sat very still, breathing quietly and staring down at the Bible which now lay on his desk. Finally he sighed deeply and got up and went to the window, drew back a small corner of the blind, and peered down into the wet streets. For a brief moment there was a silence, and Patricia and I neither spoke nor moved but kept our eyes fastened to his weary figure.

"I'm in a terrible sack," he whispered. "Yes, and you put me in it, D'Arcy. But it's my own fault for letting you put me in it." He turned to face me. "Shall I tell you? Sure, I'll tell you. Ten minutes before you brought me in, there was a very notable gathering here at Headquarters. It's too bad you missed it. Oh, yes — it was all very distinguished and everybody in the *Blue Book* and *Burke's Peerage* was here, up to and including the Police Commissioner, who rates a full page in the *Register* by himself: the Count René de Brisseaux, who is the Commissioner's particular drinking partner; the British Consul; the Eastern Seaboard Manager for Lloyd's of London; the New York representative of the London *Times* and *Manchester Guardian;* the Mayor, who was forced to leave a very attractive two-alarm fire in the Bronx; our mutual friend, the mouse Marco; and the only personality missing to make it a complete social success was Mr. God-damn D'Arcy!"

"I — I don't under — "

"Shut up!" Griffin took a small step to me, and some of the steel had returned to his voice. "You see, Mr. D'Arcy, when I heard that you and Marco were closeted in your apartment, I figured that if I got there in time you would react just as you did and open up. And the only thing that makes me hesitate about putting you on the rack right now is that I think you really believed you were telling me the truth."

I was about to affirm this vigorously, but the warning Griffin had given me was still fresh in my mind.

"But then I outsmarted myself," he continued. "Maybe that's what I get for not playing it on the square. I promised you I would let Marco go for then, but when he left your apartment, he was picked up in the lobby by Lucas and we brought him down here.

"Well . . . We gave him a little treatment and he opened up. He sang the whole scale: Helms, you, the two copies of the Aelfric Bibles in London, and the Count de Brisseaux.

"Added to what you had already told me, I was sure that this was the clutch, and so I sent out some men to the Hotel Bolton to bring in Mr. Helms and some men to bring in the Count de Brisseaux. That's where I put my head in the sack. Yes . . .

"My men came back from the Bolton. No Helms. There's a man still waiting there for him to show. The others came back with the Count de Brisseaux under their wings. The Count was very upset. I don't think my men had been very gentle or diplomatic about it, and I had warned the stupid bastards to be careful the way they handled him.

"Well, the Count let loose a lot of steaming French and demanded to call his lawyer. We couldn't stop him, and his lawyer called the Commissioner and the Mayor. Meanwhile, my call to London came through, and I spoke to Mr. Somebody at the British Museum and told him about the theft of the Bibles. He said he would check at once and call me back, and somehow it leaked out to the London *Times* and then Lloyd's of London, who insured the Bibles, were notified, and their men in New York were called and they came down along with the British Consul, who was very upset, and the Count kept screaming in French and a little in English, denying that he ever saw Marco before and didn't know what in hell we were talking about, and then Marco froze and refused to identify the Count and in comes the Commissioner and the Mayor on each other's heels just as the call from London reaches me and everybody stands and waits while I get on the phone. That's when Regan prevents me from blowing my brains out with my own gun, because the guy in London tells me, 'There's nothing to it, old boy, absolutely nothing and the Bibles are quite safe, old boy, and thanks, old boy, for your interest.' "

Griffin stopped and closed his eyes as though he were suffering exquisite pain by recalling the scene, and it was not too difficult to sympathize with his plight or become increasingly apprehensive over mine. Finally, he took a deep breath, opened his eyes slightly, and went on:

"Yes . . . that's the way it was. And that's when the Commissioner and the Mayor started to peel the skin off my stomach in wide strips, and I had to apologize to the Count and to the London *Times* and to the British Consul and to Mr. Lloyd's of London and to the Commissioner, who wants me in his office at ten o'clock this morning, and to the Mayor and to Marco, yes — to Marco. Then they all left, leaving me to my thoughts, which were not beautiful, and I've had my men out all over town looking for you and maybe it's just as well they couldn't find you right away. Now I am going to sit right here behind my desk while you tell me everything; and if you are selling stiffs to medical students or if you belong to some cult that needs dead priests and their sisters for black mass, I want you to feel that you can confide in me, that I am your friend, and that I'll understand any little strange quirk in your character."

Griffin seated himself behind the desk and fixed me with his eyes.

I leaned forward and launched into the story of Elias Behrens and the mural; and I could see that, despite himself, Griffin was impressed by the evident sincerity with which I spoke.

I told him that I had been utterly convinced of the validity of the Aelfric story when we had talked in my apartment, and that it was not until I had spoken with Patricia that I learned the real truth. This Patricia confirmed, and I placed before the detective the Behrens letter which I had taken from the girl.

Griffin read this with interest as I went on to tell him the rest; Patricia's relationship with Helms — Hekstrom — my last interview with the Reverend Probiloff at the Carlridge, and how finally I had been led to Behrens' grave in St. Francis's Cemetery.

When I had finished, I leaned back in my chair and anxiously awaited Griffin's reaction. He kept his eyes glued to the Behrens letter, then drew to himself the Bible I had found in the coffin and carefully turned the brittle pages. After a moment, he spoke to Patricia but did not take his eyes from the Book:

"This is the truth?"

"Yes."

"Do you know this Helms or Hekstrom well?"

"No. Only by reputation."

"Were you paying him well for his help?"

"Only what he asked for his time."

"And was he to share in the mural if found?"

"Why, no . . ."

"*Ummmmm.* And this mural is valuable?"

"Priceless!"

"I see . . . and he was not to share?"

"He couldn't. I didn't intend to sell it."

I got up and went to Griffin. "May I look through the Bible, Griffin?"

The detective looked up at me. "Go ahead."

Quickly I turned to the Book of Joshua. In the sixth

chapter, that which tells of the storming of Jericho, we found in the fourth paragraph these words heavily underscored, "seven priests." That was all.

I looked up triumphantly at Griffin, my finger held under the cryptic phrase.

"There it is," I said quietly.

Griffin stared at me coldly.

He said: "My job is not finding lost murals; it's finding the killer of Father Walsh and his sister."

"But the killer has the other Bible, the one for which Catherine Walsh was murdered, and to find the killer is to find that Bible — and the mural."

Griffin looked down at the Bible on his desk.

"Seven priests," he murmured. "That doesn't make much sense."

"No," I agreed, "it doesn't make sense now. But it will when we find the rest of the key in the Bible which the killer must have."

Griffin looked up at me.

"D'Arcy — who do you think has the Bible?"

"I don't know."

Griffin grunted and rose to his feet.

"I'm glad to hear that. It's nice of you to leave something for me to do." He went to the door. "Wait here. I'll be right back."

Griffin left the room, but returned in a very few minutes wearing his hat and trench coat. "Let's go."

"Where?"

"To the Hotel Bolton. I want to have a little talk with Mr. Helms-Hekstrom."

Chapter Six

THE MAN GRIFFIN had posted in the lobby of the Hotel Bolton came forward to meet us as we entered.

"No dice, Chief."

"Go back downtown. Write your report."

Griffin sought out the manager of the hotel, identified himself, and told him that he wanted to look in on the apartment occupied by Mr. Bartha, which Patricia told us was the name Helms-Hekstrom had registered under to elude Probiloff.

The manager appeared startled. "Oh, dear!" he exclaimed. "Has anything happened to Mr. Bartha?"

"Why?" asked Griffin.

"Well, he called me earlier this evening and told me that he had to leave town at once, and that he could not even stop to check out."

"Did he say where he was going?"

"No, sir. He told me that I would find his bags in his apartment, and that I was to store them until he sent for them. In fact, I was just about to go up now to supervise the removal of his luggage."

Griffin glanced at me significantly.

"Let's go, then," he said.

The manager escorted us to the apartment, while Patricia went down the hall to her own suite to take off her wet clothes.

From the appearance of the apartment, it seemed quite apparent that Helms had prepared for instant and sudden flight, but that he had been overwhelmed

99

by panic and had taken to his heels without attempting to salvage his heavy luggage.

Griffin told the manager that he could now return to his duties, but warned him that he was not to advise Mr. Bartha, should he suddenly return, that we were in his apartment. The manager nodded knowingly and left the room as Griffin turned his attention to a number of tightly packed bags and a large wardrobe trunk which stood in the spacious foyer. All were securely locked.

On the leaf of a small secretary-desk stood a portable typewriter, in it a half-finished note.

DEAR SERKO:

I find it necessary to leave town at once. I will need at least $5,000 in cash and I want you to be ready to send it to me when I again write you. I am not going to wait for the money now, but will write you again and then you

Griffin studied the note. "He was writing for money to help him in his flight," he said, "but changed his mind about it midway."

"Yes."

"He probably decided to get the money at once from this Serko — whoever he is."

"That must be Hodakis." I said. "His lawyer."

"Do you know him?"

I started to tell Griffin of my meeting with Mr. Serko Hodakis, but before I could finish there was a knock on the door, and Griffin opened it to admit the lawyer himself.

He seemed startled to find us there as he came into the room. I introduced him to Griffin.

"Sit down, Mr. Hodakis," said Griffin. "I'd like to ask you a few questions."

Hodakis slowly lowered himself into a chair, a new apprehension in his eyes. "What has — where is Mr. Helms?"

I stood by and listened carefully as Griffin questioned Hodakis.

"You are his lawyer?"

"Yes. I — But what has ... ?"

"When did you last see or speak with your client?"

"Why, late in the afternoon."

"When?"

"Yesterday, I guess you'd call it now. Yes — that was the last time I saw him, and I've been trying to get hold of him since. Earlier in the day I received a telephone call from him telling me that he must have five thousand dollars at once. You see, I handle all of his finances."

"And you gave him the money."

"Yes. I brought it up here to this apartment. Then I left. I haven't seen him since."

"And why have you come back now?"

"I was worried about him," the lawyer replied earnestly. "When I couldn't reach him by phone, I was convinced he was in some kind of trouble."

"So you decided to pay him another visit."

"Yes. I couldn't sleep. I got up and took a cab here at once."

While this exchange was taking place between the two men, I sauntered about the room, poking an idle toe against the locked bags and the trunk. I drifted over to the large closet, opened the door slightly, and peered in. I stood thus for an instant, glancing into the closet, in which were neatly hung a few suits and a hat; then I closed the door and turned my attentions back to the men, who were now on their feet.

"Well, that pretty much clinches it," Griffin was saying. "Your client is now a fugitive wanted for murder."

Hodakis stood very still, looking into Griffin's eyes. Other than blanching ever so slightly, he exhibited no reaction.

"I beg your pardon?" he said.

Griffin repeated: "Wanted for murder."

I came forward between the two men.

"No doubt about it," I said. "He was searching my apartment when Catherine Walsh came in. He struck her with the whisky bottle, took the Bible, and left. He had murdered the priest because he thought Father Walsh would turn the Bibles over to the girl — and that he wanted to prevent, hoping to gain the entire mural for himself. In fact, he had probably marked the girl for death after they succeeded in locating the painting."

"What painting?" asked Hodakis.

"Captain Griffin will explain," I said.

At Griffin's suggestion, Hodakis, as the fugitive's lawyer, consented to take care of his personal belongings at the hotel. He started to collect papers, keys to the luggage, and so forth. He moved like an automaton and seemed completely shattered.

Griffin said: "Have the luggage put in the storeroom downstairs. We'll keep a tail on it. There's always the chance that he might send for it, but I doubt it. And I'd like you to be at my office tomorrow morning."

Hodakis whispered: "Yes. I'll be there."

Griffin said: "Well, let's go. In twenty minutes, there'll be a four-state alarm out for your client. He won't get far. We'll have him in the bag before the week is out."

I said: "I'm sure you will."

My eyes were on the carpet as I spoke.

Griffin was as good as his word. That is, in so far as the four-state alarm was concerned. But days passed and Helms wasn't apprehended.

Although I succeeded in keeping Patricia's name out of it, the story about the Bibles and the Behrens 'Walls of Jericho' had, of course, broken in the press and was played up as a seven-day sensation. What with Helms somewhere in hiding with the Bible, it looked very much as if the search for the mural had struck a dead end, and a veritable epidemic of wall-scraping swept New York.

On the fourth day I received a call from Hodakis. I was in my office, trying to regain a great deal of lost ground in my work, when Susan told me that the lawyer was on the telephone. I took up the instrument from my desk, and our conversation was brief, almost monosyllabic. It ran something like this:

"Hello?"

"Mr. D'Arcy, I have very important news."

"Yes. You've heard from *him*."

Brief pause, then: "How did you know?"

"I thought that would happen."

"He has the book and —"

"Don't say too much over the phone."

"Yes. Of course. Can you come to my office?"

"When?"

"Now. He will call again. In an hour."

"I will be there."

I put the telephone away and sounded the buzzer for Susan. She came into my office with the shorthand notebook in her hand.

"Did you take that conversation, Duchess?"

She held the book aloft. "Right here, sir."

I rose to my feet and took my hat. "Good. Type it out and put in on my desk."

Susan promised she would do that at once, and I left the office to see Mr. Serko Hodakis.

"The call was from Chicago, Mr. D'Arcy. I was shocked when I heard his voice. As soon as he started to talk, I rang for my secretary and signaled her to take down the conversation. Here's a transcript."

I took the papers and glanced at the top sheet.

Tel. Conv. Serko Hodakis and Ernst Helms.
Mr. Helms Calling from Chicago. 1:04 PM.

HODAKIS: Ernst! Where are you?

HELMS: Never mind. I'm calling from Chicago. You know that. From a pay station.

HODAKIS: Ernst, what happened? You're in great trouble. Don't give yourself up in Chicago. Try to get back here and I'll —

HELMS: Be quiet! I'm not going to give myself up. Listen to me. Don't tell the police I called.

HODAKIS: I must!

HELMS: If you don't do as I ask, I'll hang up now and no one will ever hear of me again. Do you understand?

HODAKIS: But I — what do you want, Ernst?

HELMS: Call D'Arcy. Tell him I have the book. I know he has the other. Tell him I'll send you the Bible I have. Then he will be able to find the mural.

HODAKIS: But Ernst —

HELMS: Be quiet and listen! I'll send the Bible only if D'Arcy promises that my interest in the mural will be protected. You're my lawyer. You have my power of attorney. If the mural is found, I want you to represent me in any sale and I want one-half of the proceeds. One-half. I'm entitled to it. Get some kind of a legal paper from D'Arcy.

HODAKIS: But, Ernst, what good will the money do you? You're wanted for —

HELMS: I'll worry about that later. No matter what I'm wanted for, I still have a legal right to protection in a matter of this kind. You know that. And without me, they'll never find the mural. With enough money, I can do anything. Even take care of this — this trouble. Call D'Arcy. Now. Tell him to come to your office. I'll call again in an hour. If he agrees to what I want and you tell me I'm protected, I'll send the Bible at once. If not, I'll destroy it and that will be the end for everyone. Good-by.

*Connection Broken by Ernst Helms
in Chicago.* 1:08 *PM.*
(Signed) Tama Ruvetli, sec't.

I studied the conversation for a moment, then glanced up at Hodakis. The deep cleft in his upper lip and the sides of his forehead were beaded with perspiration. "I don't like it at all," he repeated, taking a silk handkerchief from his breast pocket and carefully blotting his face.

I dropped the papers on the desk. Hodakis took them and carefully locked them in a drawer.

"What do you intend to do?" I asked.

"I don't know. I can't think. I feel I should go at once to the police. What do you think, eh?"

I drew a cigarette from my case, accepted the flame offered by the lawyer, sat back in my chair, and inhaled deeply.

"Of course," I said, "if you do not report this to the police, you do run a risk of becoming an accessory. In fact, now that you've made me aware of this call, we both face that risk if we keep silence.

"On the other hand," I went on, "if we play along with Helms, the chances of apprehending him might be bettered. Right now, I am inclined to think that it would be wise to agree with him, find the mural if possible, and keep our contact with the man. Once we find 'The Walls of Jericho,' Helms might be emboldened to take more direct action. In that way it will be easier for the police to take him."

Hodakis stared down at his outstretched hands in deep and disturbed thought. The telephone rang. The lawyer hesitated, then took up the receiver. He listened for an instant, then cupped his hand over the transmitter and looked to me.

"It's my secretary. Helms is on another wire."

I nodded slowly. Again, the man hesitated, then, as though coming to a hard-reached decision, said into the telephone:

"Take this as before, Miss Ruvetli. Yes. Put him on." A small wait, then: "Ernst? Yes, he is here now. I've told him everything. Yes, he agrees. He will sign a paper giving you a one-half interest." Hodakis raised his eyes to mine, and I nodded confirmation. "Do you want to talk to him? All right, Ernst. For God's sake, be careful. I still think you should — hello, Ernst? Hello? . . ."

Apparently, the man on the other end had abruptly discontinued the conversation and Hodakis gave his secretary instructions to draw up an agreement between myself and Serko Hodakis, assuring his client a one-half interest in the mural.

"Helms promises to send the Bible to me at once," he said, putting the telephone from him. "He said I should have it in the morning mail."

I assured him I would be on hand with the other Bible, and Miss Ruvetli came in with the legal paper, which I signed, and then I rose to my feet and took my hat from the desk.

I shook his hand and left the office.

I returned to my office and called Patricia and asked her to meet me for cocktails at the St. Regis, and when I arrived at the King Cole Room I found her at one of the small tables just to the right of the entrance deep in a cocktail and conversation with Serko Hodakis.

For a moment I watched them unnoticed as they laughed at some jest the lawyer had passed, and then as they raised their drinks I sauntered up and took a seat at their table.

"I did not know you two were acquainted?" I said.

"We're not," said Patricia, and then added: "That is, not really."

"You see," explained Hodakis, "I was sitting here having my cocktail when Miss Behrens entered and asked the *maître* if you had arrived, and when I heard her mention your name, I got to my feet on impulse and rather fumblingly introduced myself —"

"Yes," Patricia cut in, "and Mr. Hodakis was kind enough to ask me to join him until you could get here."

"That was very thoughtful of Mr. Hodakis."

"Oh, not at all . . ."

"This is indeed a small world, to coin a cliché. I suppose, Mr. Hodakis, that you now know who Miss Behrens is?"

"Yes. One word led to another — you know how those things are, eh? — and I was shocked. Yes — that's the word, I was absolutely shocked when I learned of her participation in the search for the mural."

"You mean," I asked casually, "her financing of the search?"

Hodakis reddened slightly.

"Believe me, Mr. D'Arcy, this was the first I learned of that. I did not know anything about Miss Behrens till this minute, and I did not know that it was her money which was being used."

"I can understand that," I said softly.

"In fact," Hodakis continued worriedly, "this puts an entirely new light on the situation as far as I, as a lawyer, am concerned."

"I don't understand."

"I mean, your right to sign that paper giving my client that interest."

Patricia looked from Hodakis to me in some perplexity, as though she could not follow the thread of our conversation.

"I am sure," I said, "that Miss Behrens will not contest any action I might take in her behalf."

Hodakis pondered for a moment, then sighed deeply and glanced at his watch. He rose to his feet and made his farewells, and it was obvious that he was a highly perturbed individual.

When he had gone, Patricia turned to me and she made no attempt to conceal her excitement.

"What were you talking about? What paper — ?"

I made known to her the day's developments, and she concluded that the fugitive was a fool to act as he had, and she was sure that his greed would prove to be his undoing.

"Immediately after we do find the mural," I told her, "you are going to announce that you are returning at once to San Francisco and that you are taking all of the Helms-Hekstrom luggage back with you."

"No. Oh, no, D'Arcy! I don't want to go."

"I don't intend that you shall go back to San Francisco. I have other plans for you. But you will do as I say tomorrow or I shall beat you unmercifully. Come along."

N O, NO, IT HASN'T COME," said Hodakis.

His moist, nervous hands continued to search the morning mail on his desk.

"Nothing?" I asked.

"Nothing. Nothing at all."

"A letter, a note?"

"You can see. You can see for yourself. Nothing."

Patricia leaned forward to speak, but then she settled back, her body taut.

"What time is the next mail due?" I asked.

"Eleven-thirty," Hodakis said.

I glanced at my watch.

"*Ummm.* Two hours and twenty minutes."

There was a pause, and we could hear the slow, rhythmic beat of the pendulum clock in the corner.

Patricia sat stiffly in her chair, drawing her handkerchief through her fingers, her lips tight in an effort to contain herself.

"D'Arcy, I can't bear it!" she said suddenly, her voice razor-sharp. "I mean, to simply sit here this way for two hours and — I shall scream!"

"Strange — but I was just contemplating the very same thing. May I use your telephone, Mr. Hodakis?"

The lawyer nodded his permission, and I called the General Post Office. I put my inquiry and was informed that an airplane bearing mail from Chicago would arrive at 9:35, and that all pieces marked for special delivery would be distributed without delay.

We fell back into the strained, restless silence; and that silence continued to hang tensely until there was a light knock on the door and Miss Ruvetli entered the room. In her hand was a small, tightly wrapped package the size of a book, and the brown paper was covered with many stamps and postal markings. She came to Serko Hodakis's desk and placed it before him and told him that the package had just arrived via special delivery; and Hodakis stared down at the package and said, "Thank you, Miss Ruvetli," without looking up. Miss Ruvetli nodded quietly and left the office.

Patricia and I came to the lawyer's side and waited for him to open the wrapping. Neither of us spoke, but Hodakis just sat and stared at the package and did not move until I suggested that he open it, and he put his hands on the package and drew it to him.

It was addressed to him in block figures, stamped *Airmail, Special Delivery, Fee Claimed by Office of First Address.* Hodakis started to untie the twine coiled about the package, but his fingers fumbled, and without speaking he held it out to me. I took the package with one hand while with the other I sprang the tiny automatic blade of the small knife attached to my key-chain, and with the blade I cut through the light twine. I removed the brown paper, the inner protective covering of heavy cardboard, and a fair quantity of tissue paper which was beneath this. Then we saw the Bible. There was no letter, no note, no message of any kind. There was only the Bible. It was very old. On its cover were the initials *E. B.*

Still without speaking, I laid the Bible on the desk, and the others leaned forward anxiously as I carefully turned the fragile pages. I found the Book of Joshua. My eyes carefully searched through the text and there, in the fourth paragraph of the sixth chapter, as in the Bible which had been buried with Elias Behrens, two words had been heavily underscored: "seven rams."

Without removing my eyes from the page, I held out my hand and Patricia gave me the Bible we had unearthed in St. Francis's cemetery.

I opened the Bible in my hand to the sixth chapter of the Book of Joshua and the indicated words: "seven priests."

I placed the two Bibles side by side, and we studied the cryptic message. Hodakis's brow was deeply grooved. His lips formed the phrases of the Bibles, and he muttered incoherently.

For a moment, I, like the lawyer, found myself greatly mystified by the cipher, and the alarming thought of a possible hoax assailed me. But with startling abruptness, as though someone had applied a turn of the screw to the microscope, all of the abstruse indeterminates coalesced and stood in sharp focus for me to read clearly and understand in all its completeness, and a warming glow of satisfaction suffused my being.

I said: "Patricia, my pet, you will love this."

Hodakis said: "D'Arcy ... please ..."

I leaned back on my heels, closed my eyes, and relished the moment.

"Yes," I murmured. "Seven priests and seven rams." There was a definite note of complacency in my voice which I did not trouble to eliminate. "Yes, the entire secret lies in those words." I opened my eyes and gazed blandly at the lawyer. "I know where to find 'The Walls of Jericho.' "

No one moved, no one spoke, and even the *tick-tock* of the pendulum clock seemed muted.

"Elias Behrens," I went on, "was an artist. Where, in the days of his agony, would an impoverished artist find shelter, solace, and sympathetic companionship? Inevitably, would he not gravitate to the center where others of his temperament, of his art, also converged? There is a street in Greenwich Village called Ramm Street. Yes ...

" 'And seven priests shall bear before the ark seven trumpets of rams' horns ... and it shall come to pass that when they make a long blast ... the wall of the city shall fall down flat ...'

"And with the addition of the two numerals, seven and seven," I concluded, "we should find 'The Walls of Jericho,' by Elias Behrens, at 77 Ramm Street!"

Serko Hodakis came to his feet.

"Splendid, splendid! That was truly wonderful, Mr. D'Arcy! You agree to that, eh, Miss Behrens? Yes, yes, indeed!"

"One moment," I interrupted. "First, do you have something in which I could carry these Bibles, Mr. Hodakis?"

"Certainly, certainly!"

Hodakis seemed to have recovered his lusty joviality as he held out his portfolio. I placed both books in the brief case and then turned to the lawyer.

"Now, may I use your telephone?"

"Certainly, certainly!"

I took up the instrument, asked to be given an outside wire, and dialed a number. After a moment, a voice said: "Brooklyn Museum."

I said: "This is D'Arcy. I want to speak to Mr. Sheldon Keck."

While I waited for the connection, I explained to the others that Sheldon Keck was an old friend of mine, one who knew how to be discreet, and considered by the art world to be an authority on the subject of restoring defaced and repainted canvases and murals.

Keck's voice came across the wire: "D'Arcy?"

"Yes. How are you, Sheldon?"

"Excellent. What can I do for you?"

"Good Lord, Kecky," I groaned. "You practically say that I call you only when I am in need of a favor. However, this time I have something tremendously exciting, something that will set the art world — Well, never mind. I'll explain when I see you. How soon can you get into town?"

"Now?"

"At once. And I want you to bring your equipment for locating a repainted mural."

"D'Arcy," said Keck, and his voice was low with excitement, "what is — have you found the —"

"Believe me, Sheldon, the biggest thing since the recovery of the 'Mona Lisa.' That is, if it is true. I can't know until you test — so for heaven's sake, come!"

"Immediately. Where?"

"I'll be waiting for you at 77 Ramm Street."

"77 Ramm Street," he echoed.

I glanced at Patricia. "Yes," I said into the phone. "You can't miss it. There is a sign outside: Bianca's

Neapolitan Restaurant, and it is two steps below street level."

I put the telephone aside and smiled up at the girl.

"Yes, my fair one," I murmured. "I told you that you would love it. Apparently, our little friend Bianca has more than fly-specks on his walls!"

WE DESCENDED the few steps leading into the restaurant and were greeted by Bianca in his usual hearty manner.

"Meester D'Arcy! Is so good to see you again, no? What for I don' onnerstan' how you come so soon in the morning! I joost open, and Carmella he is now cook the lunch."

Bianca led us to my small table in the rear and seated Patricia on my right, Hodakis on my left. The lights had not yet been turned on, and it was pleasant being in the cool, shadow-filled room. No other diners were present.

"Bianca," I said, "I've come here so early today —because I am in search of material. I am going to write a series of articles about the older Greenwich Village dining places: their histories, stories about their owners, and so forth."

"And you will write about Bianca's Neapolitan Restaurant?"

I nodded and, highly flattered that I should choose his establishment as one of my subjects, Bianca willingly told me all he knew and all he had heard about his building.

The small house, numbered 77 Ramm Street, in which his place of business was situated had been owned by his father before him in the days when it had been merely a Greenwich Village livery stable. Bianca's ambitious father had renovated the building with his own hands and with the help of his many children, and on the upper two floors he had constructed apartments to house his extensive brood.

The basement floor, the room in which we were now seated, he had converted into a series of square rooms, each measuring fifteen by fifteen. These small apartments grew to be popular with the era's affluent artists and writers, but as time went by the elder Bianca found that his cavaransary was attracting writers and artists of less and less affluence, until finally the vanishing point was reached, and he could no longer afford to continue the enterprise.

It was at Bianca's next words that I felt my first wave of nausea, and I could see that both Patricia and Hodakis also recognized the implications when the little man told us that his father's next venture was to tear down all of the partitioning walls in the basement and establish the restaurant which Bianca himself was now carrying on for the second generation.

"Just — just a minute, Bianca," I interrupted. "You mean that there were five or six rooms in this basement?"

"That'sa right!"

"And — they each had their own walls?"

"That'sa right!"

"And — your father later tore all these walls down to open the —"

"That'sa right! That makes a good story, no?"

The door at the front of the restaurant opened, and Sheldon Keck entered. I rose to make him welcome and introduce him to Patricia and Hodakis and Bianca.

Keck seated himself at the table and placed his small bag on the floor by his feet. I sent Bianca off into the kitchen to fetch some food, and when he had gone, I quickly made known to Keck the story of the Behrens mural.

I could see in his brown eyes his mounting excitement, and then the apprehension as I continued to tell him of the destruction of the walls in the basement.

Keck leaned back in his chair, his eyes roving the walls professionally, his fingers playing nervously through his blond hair.

"Well, D'Arcy," he said at last, "our only hope is that Behrens painted the mural on one of the outer walls of the building — that is, one of the walls now standing."

"Yes . . ."

"And all I can do is test for it . . ."

Hodakis leaned forward.

"Tell me, Mr. Keck, tell me," he said, "how much would that mural be worth?"

Keck gave him one of those looks; but the lawyer, completely immersed in visions of wealth, remained insensitive.

"Well, I don't know, Mr. — er — . . ."

"Hodakis."

"Hodakis. I should say that two hundred and fifty thousand dollars would not be too much."

Hodakis inhaled sharply.

"A quarter of a million!"

Keck turned from him abruptly to face me. "Let's get to work."

While Sheldon Keck withdrew his instruments from the bag and placed them neatly on the table, I went back into the kitchen to speak with Bianca. I told him that my newly arrived friend desired to conduct an experiment on his walls, and it was evident that Bianca did not find much time to read the daily newspapers, for he could not understand. But I assured him that he would be amply reimbursed for any damage we might inflict on his property.

With his customary fervor, Bianca made me understand that he had implicit faith in me and that if I so desired I could feel free to tear his building down right about his ears and never would he question my motives. I was touched with this display of simple trust, and I promised anew that come what may, Bianca would not suffer any loss.

We went into the dining room where Bianca bolted the front door and threw into life the electric lights set into the walls — both at Keck's request. We then stood by the table on which Keck had placed his bag, and, along with the others, we watched in silent interest the expert's preparations for his work.

Ranged neatly on the cloth were four small glass jars, each containing a quantity of liquid and its identifying label; a microscope such as might be found in a medical laboratory, complete with glass slides and light bulb; a hollow hypodermic needle from which the sharp point appeared to have been clipped and the rim honed down to razor edge. The needle was of steel, about fifty millimeters in length and thirty milli-

113

meters in diameter, and, deprived of the point we expect on a hypodermic needle, it resembled in miniature the shell of an expended bullet. By the side of the needle lay an instrument about ten inches in length, not unlike the common screw driver, but terminating in a small cuplike affair which, I saw, was designed to accommodate the needle.

"There are various methods for determining if a work of art lies hidden beneath another painting, or is cloaked in any other manner," Keck explained while assembling the microscope. "There is the X-ray method, and also infra-red ray. But in a problem of this kind, where the solid wall of a building is to be tapped for a mural, the most efficient instrument is the microsectioner." Keck pointed to the needle.

"And the microsectioner," he continued, "has the added advantage of telling us exactly what materials might be covering the mural: a coat of plaster, for example — and that is something, incidentally, which I pray we do not find — that is, if we find the mural at all."

"Would a coat of plaster present difficulties?"

Keck smiled wryly.

"*Difficulties* is beautiful understatement. It would take a crew of experienced craftsmen the better part of a year, depending upon the size of the mural, to slowly chip away the plaster with those scalpels you see there. It's a tedious and highly delicate operation in which the men must be very careful not to mar the mural itself."

Keck wandered about the room, lightly tapping the pine paneling with a small hammer. Then, apparently choosing a section at random, he applied other tools and slowly and carefully pried the wood from the wall.

With a section cleared and the pine wood lying on the floor, Keck came to his work table, took up the microsectioner and slowly forced the needle into the wall. He did this with infinite care, not jarring the handle which gave him leverage, and for an instant the needle remained embedded approximately an eighth of an inch in the wall.

Painstakingly he withdrew the instrument, came with it to the table, and, holding the needle gently between thumb and forefinger, removed it from the small cup on the end of the implement, then fastened the needle to the plunger contrivance. Holding it over a glass slide, he slowly pressed a firm thumb down upon the plunger and ejected onto the slide a sliver of the wall about an eighth of an inch in length and a little less than the diameter of the needle.

He took up the slide, placed it under the lens of the microscope, and put his eye to the instrument. As he slowly adjusted the delicate controls, bringing the subject of his examination into precise focus, Keck said slowly:

"I have on the slide what is literally a miniature cross-section of the wall, and from this I can determine in perfect sequence just how the wall is constructed, whether or not there is plaster over the mural, and what paints have been applied at various times."

For a few minutes, Keck proceeded with his examination in silence. Then:

"*Ummmmm.* A layer of blue paint first," he murmured. "Which is what you now see on the wall. Under that is a layer of green, then a darker blue over flat white, then the plaster — and that's all . . ."

Sheldon Keck looked up, removed his glasses, and rubbed his eyes. The disappointment in the room hung heavy.

"What do you mean: that's all?" Hodakis leaned forward, a growing panic in his eyes. "Does that mean there's no mural, eh?"

"Not there, at any rate. I've just begun to work and there is a great deal more wall space. You needn't despair yet."

"If you should strike the mural," I asked, "what signs would you find?"

"There would be some oil tone in one of the layers of the specimen."

Keck returned to his examination of the walls, and worked without pause, tearing down paneling and taking specimens with the microsectioner. Finally, after the three hours of unremitting labor, the search having extended even into the kitchen, Keck turned to me and in his tired eyes I could read a great sympathy.

115

He shook his head slowly. "I'm sorry, D'Arcy."

I cannot now say how the others had reacted to his verdict. I had not dared to look to them. My own feeling of frustration had been so profound, I feared that should I look into Patricia's face I should not be able to restrain the tears.

I leaned back slowly, closed my eyes, and then I heard Keck's voice.

"It's a remote chance, D'Arcy. But it's a chance. Here, help me."

I opened my eyes to see Keck drawing a table to the center of the room. Without question, I took hold of the other end, and in this manner we lined up nine or ten tables, forming a hollow square about the room.

Keck took up his microsectioner once more and nimbly leaped to the top of a table which Hodakis and I held steady. He raised his arms and carefully inserted the needle into the ceiling directly overhead.

Yes, it was the ceiling. . . .

It was not until Keck was examining the fifth specimen he had taken that I noticed the sudden strain sweep across his back. I could see the muscles in his neck go taut as he leaned over the microscope, and none of us dared breathe as he made minute adjustments of the controls.

Finally, without taking his eyes from the lens, Keck spoke, his voice low and charged with emotion:

"I think . . . I don't know. . . . It looks like a flesh tone . . . oils . . ." His voice trailed off as he made a further adjustment of the lens, and then: "The surface blue, then calcimine, the third layer a pink-purple, again whitewash, the fifth layer a green, then a flat white, and under this the sixth layer is a flesh tone. I think it's oils . . ."

The sharp upsurge of emotion could be felt in the little room with the intoxicating strength of straight brandy, and Keck's smile was beautiful to see.

"Thank you, D'Arcy, for calling me." His voice was soft and fell like a feather. "I'll never forget this experience. We have found the mural. Over our heads is the last, great work of a master, 'The Walls of Jericho,' by Elias Behrens."

Patricia's fingers found my hand. I knew there

were tears in her eyes.

Bianca murmured: *"Madre mia!"* over and over.

Hodakis breathed: "God, God, a fortune!"

Keck turned back to his work table and rapidly mixed a solution with the liquids from the glass jars labeled, "acetone," "eth. alch.," "toluene." To this he added a small amount of turpentine, and, with a soft cloth in one hand and the solvent in the other, again mounted the table under the paint-covered mural.

He moistened the cloth with the mixture and then applied it to the ceiling with a gentle circular motion. Slowly, and each in its turn, there was revealed under the outer covering of blue paint a coat of calcimine, then a pink-purplish color, then more calcimine, and under this a green-colored paint applied over a flat white; and when this last flat white was slowly washed away by the solvent on the cloth there came into view a definite flesh tone.

Keck gingerly worked around and around and around this flesh tone until a face that was slightly larger than life-size began to take form, and finally we saw the entire head there on the ceiling above us. It was an imperious head, reflecting great strength and determination in its majestic lines and clear cobalt-blue eyes. This, I knew at once, must be Joshua himself standing at the head of his armies and looking down through those unyielding eyes onto the walls of the City of Jericho.

"The actual restoration," explained Keck, "will have to be done on the ceiling by a crew of craftsmen."

I thanked Sheldon Keck for his invaluable help and told him that the entire project would be under his supervision to execute as he thought best, and for this he thanked me. Then I turned to Bianca and told him that he was to have a generous share in the mural, and Bianca said that whatever I decided he would accept without question. For this I thanked him, but warned him that he must guard his tongue, that he must bolt his doors after us and permit no news of this discovery to seep forth until I was ready. He assured me he would remain as silent as the tombs and all present promised the same; and then, when Sheldon Keck had finished packing his equipment and told us he was ready to leave, I said: "Yes, we can go now," and turned to Serko Hodakis and told him that he should accompany Patricia and me to my apartment. And then we left the debris-strewn restaurant as Bianca extinguished the lights and bolted his doors firmly after us. . . .

I stood behind my small bar and mixed highballs while Hodakis took his ease in the large chair. Patricia reclined on the window seat, the rays of the bright afternoon sun shooting through her lovely hair.

"We have quite a few problems to consider," I said. "Plain water or fizz, Mr. Hodakis?"

"Fizz, thank you."

"Patricia?"

"Soda, please."

I served the drinks.

"Thank you." Hodakis took his glass. "Yes, Mr. D'Arcy, we most certainly do have a few problems. And, frankly, I don't know where to begin."

I seated myself by Patricia's side, my drink in hand.

"Well, let us consider what we have and what we have done. We have the mural. Now, we could only have the mural if we secured the second Bible from your client, who, at present, is in the unenviable position of being a fugitive wanted for murder. Therefore, if we now announce the discovery, Griffin must know at once that we have been, in some manner, in touch with the murderer. Correct?"

Hodakis stared into his drink as though he might there find the solution to the problem I had presented.

"Yes, yes . . ." he murmured.

"Then how," asked Patricia, "are we going to —"

"That, of course, is our knottiest problem. And before we discuss anything else, disposal of the mural or sharing in the proceeds, we must first devise some plan whereby we will be able to apprehend your client. We are in a very delicate position. Do you not agree, Mr. Hodakis?"

"Yes . . . but . . . I mean, I see your point, of course, and I'm afraid I was not sufficiently foresighted to anticipate this complication. It certainly *is* a complication, eh?"

I could not restrain a brief smile.

"I am inclined to agree. The point is: what's to be done?"

"See here," said Hodakis suddenly. "Why must we say we spoke with my client?"

For a moment, I must admit, I was puzzled.

"I don't understand."

Hodakis leaned forward eagerly in his chair.

"It's simple: isn't it possible — can't it be, say, that we found the mural *without* the use of the second Bible?"

"*Ummmmmm.* I see. Yes, possible. But not very probable."

"Let the police prove otherwise!"

"And they can."

"How?"

"That second Bible is in my possession."

"But who is to tell them that?"

"I."

Hodakis stared at me uncomprehendingly. Then he slowly rose to his feet.

"I don't — what are you talking about?"

"Perhaps I'd better explain," I said quietly.

"Yes. Yes," said Hodakis. "I think you'd better!"

"For various reasons," I began, "I was most eager to discover the mural. But that was not — and still is not — my primary purpose. No . . . I became involved in this nightmare for only one reason: to find the man who murdered Father Walsh and his sister Catherine. The finding of the mural I looked upon merely as a necessary step in his apprehension. Now I find that your help in the remainder is most necessary. You will either agree to do as I say, or I shall go at once to Griffin with the entire story of how the second Bible came into your possession."

Hodakis's face darkened.

"I'll swear I don't know anything about it! I'll swear I never saw that Bible!"

I turned on him sharply, and for the first time raised my voice.

"Don't be naïve! The day you telephoned to tell me of your client's call from Chicago, my secretary made a transcript of our conversation, which I now have under lock and key. Further: there is a postal record of the special delivery package which you received and for which your secretary signed, the day immediately following our conversation. And further still: I have the Bible you received in your brief case which you gave to me for the purpose of carrying it from your office. But we can, as you would say, discount all of that if you like. You seem to forget that Miss Behrens was present in your office when the Bible arrived!"

Hodakis lowered himself slowly into the chair.

"I — I'll do everything I can to help you . . ."

"Excellent. Now, when do you think your client will again call you?"

"That's hard to say. Tomorrow, the day after . . ."

"If you are in your office when he calls, instruct your secretary to tell him that you will not be in for a half-hour. Notify me. I'll want to be there when he calls back. And I'll have Griffin with me."

"Griffin?"

"Do not be alarmed, Mr. Hodakis. From now on, you will have to rely upon my judgment without question. I have a plan in mind which, I am convinced, will exonerate us of charges of conspiracy or of being accessory after the fact, and will, at the same time, enable us to take the murderer."

Hodakis blotted his brow with his handkerchief. "Well, I hope you know what you are doing."

I turned to Patricia. "But before any of this takes place, my dear, I'll want you out of the city."

"Why?"

"There is a slight chance that it might prove messy, and so far I've succeeded in keeping your name clear. Let us not jeopardize that now. I think it would be wiser for you to return to San Francisco at once."

"Oh, D'Arcy, no!"

"Don't be difficult. And you will take all of the luggage now being held in the storeroom at the Bolton which belongs to the fugitive."

Again Hodakis came to his feet.

"What's this? Why?"

"For excellent reasons, Mr. Hodakis, which I cannot now make clear to you. When your client calls, you must tell him that Miss Behrens has taken his luggage back to San Francisco, and I have a strong feeling that our last act might be played out in the shadow of the Golden Gate."

"Do you think you will be able to remove the luggage?"

"Yes . . . You will leave tomorrow morning, Patricia. We will make arrangements at once. And now I suggest we leave for our much-needed lunch. I am practically dying from lack of food."

We then left the apartment and, after we had had a brief lunch and Serko Hodakis had taken his leave of us, Patricia and I called on Captain Griffin at Police Headquarters.

We talked for about a half-hour, and I told Griffin all that had happened, including the finding of the mural and then I asked him to permit Patricia to remove the luggage from the storeroom of the Hotel Bolton and take it with her on the train to San Francisco.

Griffin thought for a moment, and said:

"*Ummmmm.* That train you'll be on, Miss Behrens; it goes through Chicago, doesn't it?"

"Yes," I said. "It does."

Griffin looked at me through his left eye.

"All right, D'Arcy. I'll play along with you."

And that is where we left it for then.

PATRICIA'S TRAIN for the west coast was due to leave Grand Central Station at 3:25; and all of her luggage, including that which was being held in the storeroom of the Hotel Bolton, was to be called for by the Railway Express Agency at noon. Thus fifteen minutes before the noon hour found Captain Griffin seated next to me in a taxi parked directly opposite the Bolton's delivery entrance on Fifty-eighth Street.

"What if he doesn't make the break?" asked Griffin.

"He will," I replied.

We lapsed into silence, and after a few minutes an American Railway Express truck rolled down the street and came to a halt before the delivery entrance. The driver nodded unobtrusively to Griffin. He was one of his special detail men.

"Yes, that's it," said the detective.

The driver and his helper leaped from the truck and disappeared inside the hotel. Within a few minutes they returned, aided by hotel porters, with a deal of luggage, including Helms-Hekstrom's, and loaded it onto the back of the truck. Then they slammed shut the huge doors and drove off slowly.

Griffin looked at me. I did not say anything. The detective ordered our driver to follow the truck, which led us far over to the east side and then south to Grand Central Station, where it rolled down the ramp and halted before the receiving platform.

Griffin and I left our taxi and followed the luggage to the baggage coach, where it was received by the railway clerks and stored safely on the train. Working with the clerks in that coach were Regan and Lucas. The two detectives had prepared a place of concealment for us. I lowered my bulk behind some massive trunks. It was very uncomfortable. Griffin was hidden not far from me. Suddenly we felt a slight jar, then the train rolled smoothly. We were on our way. Patricia, I knew, was, according to instructions, in Pullman car 10 up ahead.

For forty minutes the journey remained uneventful. Once or twice Griffin craned his neck to look at me. I looked away. He had not said anything, but I knew what he was thinking. So far, nothing, absolutely nothing, had happened.

The train began to lose speed. We were approaching Harmon. There we would stop for the engine change. The door leading into the baggage coach from the Pullmans opened. A man entered. He wore a long camel's-hair coat of the belted, wrap-around variety, and a felt sport hat. Over his eyes were dark sun glasses, the rims white bone, and in his gloved hand he carried an opened telegram. He was highly agitated.

Waving the telegram before him, he came to one of the clerks.

"See here," he said; "I must get off at once. The

122

minute we stop at Harmon. I must return to New York."

"What do you want me to do?" asked Regan.

"I just received this wire. My name is Henry J. Behrens. I'm traveling to San Francisco with my daughter. She is going on, but I must return to New York at once."

"I still don't know what you want me to do."

"My trunk. It's here somewhere. Here are my tickets. See?" He held the tickets forth and then withdrew them. "My trunk is— Yes, there it is. That one. See the name on it? Behrens."

Regan placed his hand on the Helms-Hekstrom trunk.

"This yours?"

"Yes. That one. I want it put off when we get to Harmon."

"Okay. Guess I can drop it. Sign this."

Regan produced a form book which the man hastily signed.

The train came to a complete halt. We were in Harmon. Regan and Lucas rolled back the large side door. They lowered the trunk to the station platform.

"Can I get off here without going back to the Pullman?" asked the man.

"Sure. But be careful. Step onto the trunk."

The man did as he was instructed, and then the two detectives rolled the door shut. Griffin and I came out from behind our screens.

"Open up the other side," said Griffin.

The opposite doors of the baggage coach were rolled back, and the three detectives leaped to the other side of the station. I went quickly into the train and found Patricia.

"Come along. Quickly."

We alighted just as the train got under way, and I saw Griffin and his men waiting for the long line of coaches to roll by.

The train moved out of the station and, as Patricia and I hurried to the detectives, we could now see Serko Hodakis on the other side of the tracks. He stood with his hand on the trunk, with his back to Griffin and his men. He no longer wore dark glasses.

Hodakis raised an arm to greet a man leaving an automobile parked under the station shed. It was the Reverend Sergei Probiloff. At the wheel of the car was Rauch.

I held Patricia firmly by the elbow and hurried her steps, but before we could reach the station proper, the detectives had crossed the tracks, and Griffin had placed a hand on the lawyer's arm.

There seemed little sequence or continuity in the events which followed. Probiloff halted abruptly, indecisively, a hand which might have reached for a gun suspended in mid-air; the automobile with Rauch behind the wheel suddenly went into motion and bore down upon the detectives; a shot was fired by one of the detectives; and the automobile swerved erratically and crashed into a slow-moving freight inching by the station. The car turned turtle. Rauch was pinned underneath. He was no longer an object of concern.

By the time Patricia and I reached the group, the lawyer and Probiloff had been manacled. No one spoke. It was almost like a ballet. Griffin found the key to the trunk in the lawyer's pockets. He inserted it in the lock and threw back the bolt. He lifted the lid of the trunk. Patricia turned her head away.

Wedged inside was the crumpled and bloated body of Mr. Ernst Helms-Kekstrom. He had been dead for almost a week.

"Patricia, my sweet . . ."
"Yes, pet?"
"Will you fix another drink for me?"
"But of course, angel!"

Patricia went to my small bar and mixed the highball. I glanced down at the letter on my desk which I was composing.

It had been late when we arrived in New York from Harmon, and both Patricia and I were exhausted. I told Griffin that we would stop at my apartment to freshen up a bit, and then come to headquarters where I would tell my story. To this Griffin had agreed, and while he and his men took Serko Hodakis and the Reverend Probiloff downtown, we had come to my place. But during the half-hour since we had arrived, both Patricia and I lost all desire to visit Headquarters that night. Hence the letter . . .

Patricia brought my drink and placed it before me.

"Taste that, sweet, and tell me if it's all right."

I sipped the highball. "Like you, my lovely, perfect."

"Darling . . ."

"Take a drink, sit on that couch and I will join you in less than three minutes."

Patricia reluctantly did as I advised, and I returned to the letter:

My Dear Captain Griffin:

Circumstances over which I do not wish to exercise any control make it delightfully impossible for me to visit with you this evening at Headquarters. Since I know, however, that you are most eager to hear from me (as who is not?) this note will be dispatched via special messenger and will serve the purpose of answering any and all questions you might wish to ask. It is not that I do not enjoy your company. Indeed, there are moments when you are almost amusing. But tonight I — well, I am sure you understand. Therefore, I shall be brief, concise and very much to the point:

My first inkling that something was very wrong with Mr. Serko Hodakis came when I found Patricia Behrens trussed up in the Reverend Probiloff's apartment. She told me that Probiloff had vehemently demanded that she and the late Mr. Helms-Hekstrom give to him the Bible which he insisted, despite her protests, they had in their possession. But she did not have a Bible, and neither did Mr. Mr. H-H. And the only man in New York who should have been under that strong impression that they did have a Bible was Mr. Serko Hodakis. Why? Because that very afternoon, for my own devilish purposes, I had lied to him and told him that I had delivered to Mr. H-H one of the Bibles. By this lie I unwittingly signed Mr. H-H's death warrant, and damned near Miss Behrens's.

Yes, Mr. Hodakis and the Rev. Probiloff were working in concert. The lawyer had known all along, of course, what Helms-Hekstrom was searching for, but he also knew that his client was a sincere and reputable art dealer and there would be very little personal profit for anyone should he succeed in finding the mural. Mr. H-H was in the search because of his love of art, and his only charge to Miss Behrens was for his time and efforts. This, however, did not square with Mr. Hodakis's ideas at all, and so he tipped off the unscrupulous Probiloff and kept him advised of the progress of the search being made by Miss Behrens and his client.

The enclosed note, which I found while searching the Rev. Probiloff's apartment and which advises the bogus Reverend to come from Chicago to New York at once, is the work of Serko Hodakis. You can see that in this note, he tells Probiloff that Mr. H-H ("the little man is hot") had traced the Bibles to a priest named Father W.

Then later, on the very same night on which I had found Miss Behrens in the Rev. P's apartment, you and I visited Mr. H-H's apartment in the Hotel Bolton, and from what we saw there it seemed evident that Mr. H-H had taken to his heels. The call to the manager of the hotel, purportedly from H-H, had been made by Hodakis — just another straw to point to flight on the part of H-H.

The note in the typewriter (Hodakis's work, of course) asking his lawyer for money seemed to make that a certainty. Then Hodakis appeared. He was shocked to find us there because he had come at that hour to order removal of the trunk in which he and Probiloff and Rauch had placed Mr. H-H's small body. When I looked into the closet while you were questioning Hodakis, I saw a number of suits. The trunk was tightly locked. Those suits should have been in the trunk. But instead, as we know, there was no room in the trunk for such mundane things as clothes.

Then I recalled my first telephone-conversation with Serko Hodakis. It was on the day when Catherine Walsh was murdered in my apartment. He made a point of asking me exactly where I was, and then insisted that we meet at once. When I told him it would take me about an hour to reach his office, he seemed singularly pleased. When I arrived at his office, he was not there. His secretary told me that he had gone out for a few minutes to the Magistrate's Court and would soon return. But I later recalled that, at the time I had arrived at his office, the courts were closed for the day.

Finally, he arrived — and he had been gone long enough since the time I talked with him on the telephone to have visited my apartment to search for a Bible, been surprised by the entrance of Catherine Walsh, and then murdered her with the whisky bottle. When he came into his office he was carrying a brief case. In that case was the Bible for which he had killed Catherine Walsh. The case is now in your possession, the one which I borrowed to carry the Bibles.

Father Walsh had been murdered by Rauch and Probiloff. Hodakis knew that Patricia was to see the priest that night. He told Probiloff they must prevent the old man from giving the Bibles to the girl. They arrived shortly before I did and, while Rauch held the old man aloft, Probiloff quickly looped the cord about his neck and strung him up to the beam. That is why you found no marks of violence or finger pressures on the priest's throat. They simply hanged him, quickly, quietly, efficiently.

It was Probiloff, of course, who had called the lawyer from Chicago, posing as H-H for my benefit; and it was he who sent the Bible from that city, the one for which Hodakis had killed Miss Walsh. But there, again, the too-clever lawyer blundered. In the conversation which Hodakis had with Probiloff in Chicago, the secretary's transcript reported it as speaking with Mr. Ernst Helms. If it really had been Helms, he would have identified himself to his lawyer by his correct name: Olaf Hekstrom. But Hodakis, of course, had no way of knowing that I had already succeeded in learning the man's true identity.

Immediately after Probiloff sent the Bible from Chicago, he followed it to New York and was here in the city when we discovered the mural. Hodakis told him that some kind of a trap was being prepared to be sprung when the train with the trunk reached either Chicago or San Francisco. At any rate, they must remove the trunk before it could be opened. The lawyer was in too deeply. It was then that their desperate plan was decided upon, and Probiloff was to meet Hodakis in Harmon where the trunk would be dropped.

Well, that sums up my saga, and I am inclined to think that if you give Mr. Hodakis a slight "treatment" he will speak freely.

Yr. obed. Servant,
D'Arcy

The telephone rang. I looked up from the letter. It rang again, and then I answered. It was Griffin. Why were Patricia and I not at Headquarters? I told him we were not coming to Headquarters, that I was sending a letter explaining all.

"You see, Patricia and I— Well, we have some unfinished business to take care of before morning."

I put the telephone aside and started back to my desk, but Patricia's hand caught my wrist en route, and she pulled me down onto the couch.

The unfinished business was properly and satisfactorily taken care of before morning.

THE END